FOSTER LOVE

Janis Reams Hudson

A KISMET™ Romance

METEOR PUBLISHING CORPORATION
Bensalem, Pennsylvania

First Printing February 1991.

ISBN: 1-878702-28-9

Printed in the United States of America.

This book is lovingly and respectfully dedicated to one of the strongest, kindest, most caring, most courageous women I've ever known; a true heroine; a woman who believed in me, who encouraged me to write; the most wonderful mother-in-law any son's wife could ask for . . . to Mae, with love. We miss you.

JANIS REAMS HUDSON

Janis Reams Hudson blesses the day she decided to become a writer. She also blesses her husband and both their families for their encouragement and unflagging support of a career decision she's never regretted. A former broadcast television executive, she lives on ten rural acres in Central Oklahoma with her husband and a wild assortment of barnyard pets.

ONE

Morgan Foster didn't even try to control the rage in his voice. "Where the hell are my children?" he demanded.

"So you're Foster," the old man behind the desk said calmly. "I'm Benson, your new boss. Welcome home. And by the way, what are you doing out of the hospital?"

Morgan ignored the greasy, slick voice as he placed ten fingertips on the desktop and leaned into Benson's face. Anger boiled through his veins. "I'll ask you one more time. Where are my children?"

"Sit down and I'll tell you," Benson offered. Then, "Sit down before you fall down. You look like hell."

Morgan closed his eyes, took a deep breath, and slowly straightened while counting to ten. It took every ounce of willpower he possessed to keep from hauling the new bureau chief up off his soft, padded chair and smashing in the old man's face.

I've been back a whole damn week, he thought,

forcing himself to sit in the oversized plush chair facing the oversized, cluttered desk. *And they've been lying to me the whole damn time.*

He and his partner were only supposed to have been under cover in Central America for six months. Instead, it had lasted four years, and his *partner* had turned out to be a double agent, working for the communist-backed government of the tiny, war-torn nation. For the first three years, Morgan had held his breath, waiting for his cover to be blown, until finally, it was. It took him months after that to work his way from one hiding place to the next, until he'd finally worked his way out of the country.

Unfortunately, that had only landed him in another hotbed of civil war in the next country, and the one after that.

It took him a year and a half to get home.

The first thing he'd asked about was his kids. They'd told him they were fine, he'd see them soon, then they'd slapped him into the hospital and expected him to stay there, just because he happened to have a couple of holes in his hide.

This morning he'd got fed up with the stall tactics and walked out of the hospital. When he got to his ex-wife's house in the exclusive Washington, D.C., suburb, intent on seeing his children for the first time in over four years, he met only strangers. Even the neighbors were strangers. No one around had ever heard of Joyce Foster or her four children.

Now he focused his eyes on the man behind the desk. Benson had taken charge of the bureau only a year ago. Morgan knew absolutely nothing about him and wasn't inclined to learn anything at the moment. All he wanted was to know where his kids were. "I'm waiting," he growled.

Benson nodded. "First let me assure you that your children are fine."

Morgan clenched his jaw and waited. It wasn't like him to let his emotions show, but these were his children, damnit! Just because someone higher up in the organization trusted Benson didn't mean Morgan had to trust him.

"Did you know your wife was pregnant at the time of your divorce?"

Morgan froze. His muscles locked, his breath halted, his heart stopped. *Pregnant? Again?*

"Sorry. I can see you didn't. Let me be the first to congratulate you on the birth of your daughter, Angie." Benson flipped open a file on his desk. "She just turned four."

Something snapped inside Morgan. He slumped back against his chair. *Another daughter! Angie.* He cleared his throat. "Where are they?"

"Oklahoma."

"What?" Morgan shouted, coming upright in the chair. "What the hell are they doing in Oklahoma?"

"It's a long story, Foster. And not a very pleasant one, I'm afraid."

"You said my kids were fine."

"They are, I assure you."

"Then what is it you're not telling me?"

Benson pursed his lips and tossed the file aside. "All right, I'll give it to you straight. A year after the divorce, your ex-wife remarried. She and her new husband and your five children moved to Oklahoma City. A year later, Joyce and . . . I forget his name. It's in here somewhere,'' he said, waving toward the file. ''Well, a year after they married, the two of them, well . . . there was an accident. Late at night, ice on the roads, a semi out of control. They never knew what hit them. Both died instantly. Your children were not in the car. They're fine.''

Morgan closed his eyes and leaned his head back. Joyce, dead? True, there were no deep feelings left between them by the time they'd divorced. They hadn't parted as friends, exactly, but not enemies, either. More like acquaintances. It was hard to imagine her dead.

He tried to summon up the grief he knew he should feel, but it wasn't there. He'd been surrounded by every imaginable kind of death for four years. At least hers had been quick.

But how had her death affected the children? Who was taking care of them? Before he could ask, Benson spoke.

''Since neither you nor any other relative could be reached, the State of Oklahoma took custody of your children. They're in a foster home.''

''A *what?*'' Morgan bellowed, erupting from the chair.

''Coop said you wouldn't be pleased.''

Morgan's eyes narrowed to deadly slits in his hard face. His voice came out in a deceptively soft hiss. ''You let my kids be placed in a foster home?''

Benson met him stare for stare. ''You want any

more answers out of me, Foster, you better sit back down."

Morgan remained standing. "You let my kids be placed in a foster home?" he repeated, this time more loudly.

Benson shrugged. "First of all, it wasn't me who let anything happen. That was two years ago. I wasn't with the agency then. Second, there really wasn't much choice. At least they're all together. Coop personally checked out the couple, a Gary and Sarah Collins. According to him, they're good people, and they're taking good care of the children."

"I'll just bet they are." Even knowing that Coop, his best friend from the army, had checked things out didn't mitigate Morgan's anger. He felt like ripping something to pieces.

"They live on a small family farm in rural central Oklahoma," Benson said. "He's an accountant and commutes to Oklahoma City. She stays home and takes care of the farm and the kids. They can't have children of their own. They were glad to take in five homeless children. And they were the only ones in the state willing to take in all five of them. If it hadn't been for the Collinses, your children would have been split up for the past two years."

"Don't try to soft soap me, Benson. If you've read my file, you know I have first-hand knowledge of foster parents and farms, among other things.

"I'll just bet they were pleased to get their hands on five able-bodied kids to do all the chores for them, not to mention the money the state pays them. I know exactly how foster homes work. I grew up in nearly a dozen of them, damnit. They not only get free slave labor, they get paid, too. And if a kid is old enough to have a job, they get his salary on top of everything else. Don't tell me about foster homes."

Benson sighed and rubbed a palm across his face. "These people aren't like that, Foster. After your debriefing, I'll put you in touch with them and you can see for yourself."

"Debriefing, hell! Anything I might have had to report is years old now. I'm going after my kids."

"We need to know what's happening in the countries you came through on your way home. And there are some things you'll want to know, too."

Morgan hesitated. "Like what."

"Like your former partner, Garcia, was killed two months ago."

"That's the first good news I've had in years. What else?"

"When we got word on Garcia, we sent Coop in to locate you. We're trying to get word to him now that you're back."

Morgan nodded. He wouldn't worry about Coop. Coop could take care of himself. But his kids—his kids needed him.

"I'll make you a trade," Benson offered. "You tell us what we need to know about those other countries, and I'll give you a map so you can find your kids."

Morgan snorted. "I'm supposed to spend the

next several days, weeks maybe, satisfying your curiosity, while my kids stay in the hands of strangers, forced to do God knows what kind of work just so they can eat scraps from the table? I don't think so." He leaned a hip against the desk and almost smiled. "I'll make you a trade," he offered. "You tell me exactly how to find my kids, and I'll put everything you want to know in writing, including what I know about Garcia and his associates, and mail it to you."

"Unacceptable."

Morgan straightened. "Then I'll find them myself, and you can go whistle for your information. I quit, Benson." He turned and headed for the door.

He was halfway down the hall when Benson's voice stopped him. "Go see a man named Tom Cartwright, Oklahoma Department of Human Services, Child Welfare Division. Oklahoma City. I'll tell him you're coming."

Morgan nodded silently, then turned to go. Benson's voice called out again. "My report?"

Without slowing his steps or turning around, Morgan answered over his shoulder. "You'll get it. But I still quit. I'll let you know where to send my four and a half years' back pay."

Morgan steered the rented car off the two-lane pavement onto a dirt road, following Tom Cartwright. They'd left the Interstate a half hour ago, and a sign a while back proclaimed they were in Lincoln County, Oklahoma. They'd turned east at what was apparently *the* stop light in a town called Meeker, and now headed north again.

The countryside was dotted with property of every description, from tumble-down shacks, to family farms with green fields of alfalfa and greener pastures dotted with cattle of every imaginable color, to fancy horse ranches. Morgan had grinned when he passed a Baptist church with a misspelled sign out front, then laughed at the next church—it had outhouses in back, for crying out loud.

A moment later he'd laughed so hard he'd nearly driven off the road. The county work crew—or whoever had painted the fresh stripes on the highway—had failed to scrape the wildlife remains from the road. They'd painted their bright yellow center stripe right smack up the back of a squashed, dead skunk.

Morgan laughed again just remembering it. Then he quieted. The laughter felt strange. Foreign. He couldn't remember the last time he'd found anything to laugh about. The thought was sobering.

And he knew in his gut that the conditions his children had been forced to endure these past two years—conditions he was about to see first hand—were going to sober him even more.

The dust was so thick he had to slow down on the dirt road and fall farther behind Cartwright. It was that, or choke to death, even with the windows up.

To top it off, the dust was orange. So was the road. He shook his head. He'd been in the jungle too long, where the soil was rich and black and moist. He knew Oklahoma had red dirt, even though he'd never seen it before. He'd been to Georgia. That was close enough.

But this wasn't the deep red of the Georgia clay. This was plain, bright orange. Pumpkin orange.

His knuckles white from his tense grip on the steering wheel, Morgan wondered how much farther the Collins place was, and what he'd find when they got there.

He'd had to use every government connection he had and every threat of federal investigations and interference he could think of to get anyone to talk to him about his children. It finally took a phone call to Washington to verify his story, but in the end, they told him what he wanted to know, and Cartwright even volunteered to take Morgan to his children.

Cartwright had tried to reassure him about how well off his children were, then had sabotaged his own efforts by telling him that Mr. Collins had died right after he and his wife had taken the kids in to live with them. Mrs. Collins had been caring for them herself for nearly two years now.

That was supposed to reassure him? Fat chance. Some lady farmer, widowed, trying to run a farm alone. Of course she'd kept the kids with her. How else would all the work get done? She probably needed the extra money the state paid her, too.

Reassured, he wasn't.

The dusty orange rutted road ended at a cross road. Morgan followed Cartwright as the man turned right, then left, then turned in at the first driveway. The two-story, white frame house sat on a slight, lush, bermuda-covered rise a couple of hundred yards from the road. The drive curved around to the south side of the house, where he and Cartwright parked behind a green station wagon and a red pickup.

When they got out of their cars, two big German shepherds couldn't decide whether to bark at them, or whoever was doing all the shrieking behind the house. One dog ran up and got a pat from Cartwright, then took off around the corner of the garage. Morgan and Cartwright followed, and when they rounded the corner, Morgan halted in mid-stride.

The backyard was full of children of all ages. Laughing, shrieking children. Dark-haired, dark-eyed children. His children! A lump the size of an apple rose in his throat. His vision blurred as a dozen different emotions swamped him. He blinked rapidly, nearly overwhelmed by the mixture of joy and sorrow, love and regret, rushing through him.

He was glad no one had spotted him yet. He needed time to get himself together. They'd grown so much! Wes was nearly as tall as he was now. And the twins! Rob was a full head taller than Connie. When had that happened? Lord, they were twelve already. Then there was little Jeff, the youngest. Not so little anymore. He was tall for an eight-year-old.

He wasn't the youngest, either. Was that adorable little angel ducking behind the wheelbarrow *his?* Was that his Angie? With that long black hair and those laughing brown eyes, she had to be. She looked exactly like Connie had at that age.

Morgan whispered a silent prayer of thanks for having found his family again.

He sobered immediately. Would any of them even know him? Wes would, and surely the twins. But Jeff had been so young when he'd left. And Angie had no reason to know him at all.

Four whole damn years. Wasted!

And who was the sixth one? A teenage girl about Rob's height squatted next to Angie. She wore tight jeans, a loose T-shirt, and a long, honey-gold ponytail. Wes's girlfriend? He'd be fifteen by now. Old enough for girlfriends.

Morgan blinked the moisture from his eyes again and nearly laughed out loud when Wes plastered the girl—the one with the ponytail—in the chest with a tomato. With a start, he realized all six of the kids were involved in a juicy tomato fight. There wasn't one of them, including little Angie, who wasn't wearing at least one glob of goo and seeds.

The Widow Collins would probably have a fit when she found out what was going on. But she wouldn't be able to do a damn thing about it, because Morgan was here to take his family away from her questionable influence.

It had started innocently enough, Sarah thought with a grin. The kids had been helping her pick tomatoes and green beans, and all she'd done was toss a tomato to Wes. Just because he hadn't been expecting it, well . . . was it her fault it splattered against his collarbone?

Wes had simply laughed it off. Or so she'd thought at the time. But when she'd turned her back and bent over to pick another fruit hanging low on the plant, he'd plastered her a good one right on her hip pocket.

All hell broke loose then as the harvesting turned into a full-fledged free-for-all, moving from the garden into the back yard. Even the dogs got involved, trying to catch tomatoes in the air as the red fruit hurled toward some unsuspecting back.

Angie hid behind the wheelbarrow, which, since it held a bushel basket full of tomatoes, gave her the most ammunition. At four, she couldn't throw as hard or far as her brothers and sister, but she didn't have to. They all had to come to the wheelbarrow for ammunition, and she just waited until they were within range of her short little arms.

Sarah tried to crouch down beside her, but just then Wes caught Sarah full in the chest with a large, slightly overripe tomato.

"Wesley Dean Foster, I'll get you for that!" she shrieked. She picked out a big, soft, mushy tomato, and Wes ran. She jumped the wheelbarrow, and when he laughed at her, running backward away from her, she let fly.

Wes dove sideways, and Sarah heard Jeff holler, "Look out!"

She hadn't seen the stranger standing behind Wes, but it was too late now. He ducked and brought an arm up in front of his face. The missile exploded on impact with his bare forearm. Juicy red shrapnel bombarded his beige, short-sleeved sweater and dribbled down the left leg of his brown slacks.

Sarah's eyes widened; she covered her mouth

with both hands. *Oh, my.* Whoever he was, she hoped his clothes were washable. She also hoped he had a sense of humor. He sure had quick reflexes. And nice muscles. And beautiful, thick, straight black hair. And deep, dark eyes that sent a shiver of something hot and exciting down her spine. Eyes that were . . . familiar, somehow.

She dropped her hands from her mouth and glanced briefly at the man with him. What was Tom doing here, and who was his extremely sexy friend? Her eyes slid back to the stranger like steel filings to a magnet. She grinned at him and shrugged an apology.

He had the oddest look on his face. He didn't seem at all angry that he'd just been plastered with a ripe tomato. He seemed more curious. Stunned even. And . . . familiar. Did she know him from somewhere?

Then, unbidden, it came to her. She'd never seen him before, not actually. But she'd seen those eyes in five other faces. Younger eyes; more innocent eyes; but the same eyes. Even as the blood drained from her face, she tried to deny who he was. But she couldn't. She felt light-headed and dizzy, and her first thought was, *No! Make him go away!*

She instantly knew how selfish the thought was, but she couldn't help it. She felt sick to her stomach when she heard the sheer, unadulterated joy in Wes's voice.

"Dad!"

The tall, dark-skinned boy flung himself into the waiting arms of the only slightly taller, dark-skinned man. Sarah's eyes were riveted to that pair of hard, muscled arms wrapped tightly around the boy she thought of as her oldest child.

She raised her eyes and tried to hate the man. But the emotion she saw on his face was her undoing. The twins ran to him, and Morgan Foster included them in his embrace.

Through the turmoil of her own feelings, Sarah noticed that Jeff stood back, hands in pockets, shoulders hunched. Did he not recognize his father? He looked at her, his eyes asking what to do. With her heart breaking in two, she motioned for him to go to his father. When he did, the man scooped him up in one strong arm while still hugging the other three.

That only left Angie. Where was she? Sarah looked around and spotted the child kneeling behind the wheelbarrow, head cocked to one side while she watched her brothers and sister crowd around the stranger.

Sarah's very soul ached for the little girl who'd never seen her own father. Every little girl needed a father. Especially this one, who'd lost so much already in her short life. First her mother and stepfather, then Gary, whom Angie had immediately clung to when the kids first came to live on the farm.

Sarah knew what she had to do. But oh, God, why did it have to hurt so much? Steeling herself, trying to breathe through constricted lungs, Sarah went to Angie and picked her up.

"Come here, baby," she whispered, her voice

and hands shaking. "Let's go meet your daddy, shall we?"

"Is that man really my daddy?"

Sarah looked down into big, questioning brown eyes and tried to smile. "Yes, sweetheart, he's really your daddy."

She nearly choked on the words. How was she supposed to get through this? How was she supposed to simply hand this child into the arms of a stranger?

In the end, she handed Angie to Wes, who had turned to look for his smallest sister.

Angie gazed steadily into the tear-filled eyes of the man before her. She studied him like she would something she'd never seen before. Like the first time she'd seen cooked asparagus. Closely. Carefully. Not quite sure what she was supposed to do with it, or now him. "Are you my daddy?" she finally asked.

Morgan Foster swallowed hard and blinked several times. The look of tenderness in his eyes sent Sarah's tears overflowing. She didn't hear his answer. She couldn't stand anymore.

This man had come to take her children away from her. She saw it in his face, in the way he held them, kissed them, the way he cried unashamedly.

True, they weren't children of her body. But they were the children of her heart.

And he'd come to take them away.

A shadow fell across her face, separating her from the hot afternoon sun. She shivered at the loss of warmth. A hand touched her arm. "Sarah?"

Sarah stared at the happy, chattering group another moment, their conversation nothing more than a loud buzzing in her ears, then tore her gaze away. "Hello, Tom." Her voice came out in a croak. *Why did you bring him here?* her mind screamed.

"You okay?"

She cleared her throat and wiped her cheeks with the back of one trembling hand. She thrust her chin out and refused to look into his friendly, caring eyes. "Am I supposed to be?"

Tom Cartwright sighed heavily. "No," he said softly. "I guess not." He took a deep breath and shifted his weight from one foot to the other. "I'm sorry to spring him on you like this. He's got some sort of connections high up. The department ordered me to bring him here. But we knew from the beginning . . ."

"Yes," she whispered. "We knew. Is that supposed to make it easier?"

Tom cleared his throat nervously.

"Excuse me," Sarah said, turning her back on him and the others. "I've got to get what's left of these tomatoes in out of the sun." With stiff, jerky movements, she walked to the wheelbarrow and grasped the handles of the basket resting in it. She stood there a long moment without moving.

What was the point? Why bother canning, when she still had some of last year's tomatoes on a shelf in the cellar? Besides. There wouldn't be anyone but her to eat them now.

She tried to swallow, but it hurt too much. Somehow she had to hold herself together for the sake of the children. She couldn't let them see what their leaving was doing to her. They probably hadn't fully realized yet that they were leaving.

In an unconscious move, she let go of the basket and grabbed the handles of the wheelbarrow, then wheeled it toward the back gate. She'd feed the tomatoes to the chickens. At least *they* weren't running out on her.

At the gate, she stopped. When had she become so selfish and petty? It was something new in her personality, and she didn't much like it. Those children needed their father. They needed a permanent home, one they knew would always belong to them. No fear of being shuffled around from stranger to stranger.

He was their father, and he very obviously loved them. If he'd been gone for four years, it must have been unavoidable. Surely he wouldn't leave them again, now that he was all they had.

Morgan couldn't take his eyes off the beautiful little child, his own flesh and blood, whom he'd never seen before. He wanted to grab her and hold her and smother her with kisses. But she looked like one wrong move would send her running. Apparently she wasn't too sure about this daddy business.

The child wriggled down Wes's side and stood before Morgan, her eyes big and round, uncertain . . . accusing. "Wessy says when our daddy comes he's gonna take us away. Are you gonna take us away?"

Morgan knelt before her and smiled. "Would you like that, Angie?"

"No!" she cried, throwing her arms around Wes's leg.

Morgan reeled as if he'd been slapped. All sound stopped, except the wind. What had he expected? He was a stranger to her. He looked from face to face. The twins looked confused; Jeff looked like he was going to cry. Morgan couldn't read Wes's expression at all, and that bothered him more than anything.

"Are you . . ." Wes paused to clear his throat. "Are you home for good, Dad?"

Morgan searched his oldest son's face, wondering what lay beneath that blank look. "Yes," he answered softly. "I'm home for good. I've left the agency. No more traveling, unless we all go together."

Wes's expression relaxed with a smile.

"Sarah, too?" Jeff asked timidly.

"Sarah?" Morgan's mind went blank. *Who's Sarah?*

He was saved from answering by Wes. "Where'd she go?"

Angie turned and pointed at the one Morgan had at first thought was Wes's girlfriend, until she'd plastered him with that tomato and he'd looked into her eyes. That's when he'd realized she was no girl, but a woman. A vibrant, blue-eyed, attractive woman.

It hit him then like a brick in the chest. Sarah. Sarah Collins! *That* was his children's foster mother? That sexy, tomato-throwing tomboy?

Before he could gather his scattered wits, Wes sprinted away and headed toward the woman who was pushing a wheelbarrow out the back yard gate.

"Sarah! Wait up!" Wes called.

Sarah dropped the wheelbarrow just outside the gate and hurriedly wiped the moisture from her cheeks. She shooed the dogs back into the yard and turned to wait for Wes.

"Where're you taking the tomatoes?"

She turned and lifted the handles again. "To the chickens."

"How come? I thought we were gonna can them?"

She just shrugged and kept pushing the wheelbarrow. "There's still plenty from last year, and there'll be plenty more to can later."

Wes matched her steps and tried to look in her eyes. "What's the matter, Sarah?"

She couldn't answer. She couldn't talk past the ache in her throat.

"It's because Dad's here, isn't it." He made it into a statement, not a question.

"Don't be silly," she denied. "It's what you've always wanted, for your dad to come home. I'm glad for you."

And she meant it. She was glad for him. For all five of them. But, oh God, she never knew being glad could hurt so much. She took a deep breath and moved on to practical matters. "Why don't you kids take your dad and Tom into the house and get them some iced tea? You boys could jump in the shower and get rid of the tomatoes. When I get back, the girls and I will do the same."

Wes nodded and turned to go. Out of habit, Sarah added, "Don't use all the hot water."

There was another thing she wasn't going to have to worry about anymore. Someone else using all the hot water.

Her list was growing.

A smaller garden.

Less canning.

All the hot water I want.

She dumped the tomatoes in the chicken yard, then jumped back to escape the frantic flapping and squawking as the hens attacked their treat.

When she got back to the house she slipped in through the kitchen to avoid running into anyone. The boys were already out of the upstairs shower, and the girls were in the downstairs master bath waiting for her.

Angie and Connie were both quiet and subdued. Sarah knew she should talk to them, get them to talk, but she couldn't. She was too grateful for their lack of questions just now.

In a matter of minutes both girls were showered, dressed, and gone, leaving the bathroom to Sarah. She put on clean jeans; no sense getting fancy. She grabbed the top T-shirt from the stack of clean laundry, then tossed it aside. This wasn't exactly the best time to wear the one Wes bought her last fall after she accidentally hit him in the back of the head with the broom. It fit well, and the pale-yellow fabric suited her coloring. But she didn't think Morgan Foster would be amused by the black lettering that boldly proclaimed, "I Beat My Kids."

She settled on a plain blue shirt, then combed out her hair and studied her reflection in the mirror. A wry grin twisted her mouth. Who'd have thought that at the age of thirty-two, she'd have hair that was finally in style. Honey-gold and hanging halfway down her back, those silly little wrinkles and curls were popular at last. At least among teenagers. How many parents had been forced to buy those electric crimpers last Christmas so their daughters could wear the latest hairstyle?

A little makeup would cover up those freckles on her nose, and mascara would thicken her lashes. But never mind. She'd hidden in the bathroom long enough. It was time to go out and face the music.

When she entered the living room, Morgan Foster and Tom both stood. She noticed an absence of tomato on Mr. Foster, but his clothes still told the tale. Tom cleared his throat nervously and introduced them.

"I've . . . heard a lot about you," she managed, forcing herself to offer her hand. When Morgan took it, his grip was firm and warm. His calloused palm and fingers sent shock waves shooting up her arm. Her eyes flew to his, widened, then darted away.

He felt it, too. It was there in those deep-brown eyes. Shock. Awareness. Then, denial.

She tugged her hand free and willed her heartbeat to slow. A blush stung her cheeks when she realized five pairs of eyes watched anxiously. Six, counting Tom.

"Well." Tom's voice boomed into the silence of the room. "I've got to be going back to the city."

"You won't stay for supper?" Sarah asked frantically. He wasn't going to just leave her, was he?

"You gotta make a report on us?" Jeff asked the man.

Sarah cringed. The kids had a running joke with Tom, playfully trying to convince him how abused they were. It was all done in fun, to tease Sarah, and Tom knew that. But their father might not think it was so funny.

"That's right," Tom said with his usual smile. "Gotta make that report." Then, as if Sarah didn't have enough problems, he fell into their usual routine. "Got anything I need to add?"

The kids immediately jumped into the game, each one shouting out all Sarah's terrible deeds since his last visit.

"She still makes us brush our teeth every night."

"Yeah, and mornings, too!"

"And we have to clean our own rooms."

"Yeah. That's not fair. I mean, we're only kids, ya know."

"And don't forget the tomatoes."

"Yeah. First she made us pick 'em—"

"Then she threw 'em at us. Is that any way to treat kids?"

"And now we can't even eat what's left, cuz she fed 'em to the chickens."

"Yeah. The eggs'll probably taste like tomatoes now."

Sarah kept her eyes glued on Morgan Foster as he watched the show his children put on. His gaze narrowed, moving from child to child. There was no way he could possibly misconstrue what was going on. The kids were all laughing, and so was Tom. Foster couldn't be taking any of this seriously.

So why did he look like he wanted to hit something? Or someone?

If she could have read his thoughts just then, she'd have been surprised. Morgan certainly was. Jealousy was something new to him. He didn't like the feeling, but it wouldn't go away. The joking his kids were doing about the widow's treatment of them showed their obvious affection for the woman, and their trust in and friendship with Cartwright.

These were strangers to him, but not to his kids. Even Angie was animated as she complained dramatically about having to tie her own shoes.

Cartwright claimed he had all the complaints he could handle for one report, then asked Morgan and Sarah to walk him to his car.

Outside, out of earshot of the children, Tom didn't mince words. "I know you two would like to get this thing settled as quickly as possible."

"What's there to settle?" Morgan demanded. Sarah blanched at the harshness of his tone. "They're my children."

"Yes, Mr. Foster," Tom went on. "They're your children. That's not in question. But legally speaking, they're still wards of the state and still in the temporary custody of Mrs. Collins. They'll be wards of the state until a judge signs papers giving you custody. The state would like to have the children remain with Sarah until that time. It should only take a couple of days."

"I haven't seen my kids in over four years, and you expect me to just walk off and leave them with some stranger because of some lousy, damn piece of paper?"

"Sarah's not exactly a stranger to your children, Mr. Foster," Tom reminded him. "She's—"

"Tom," Sarah interrupted. "I know what you're trying to do, and I thank you." He was trying to delay the children's leaving as long as possible. He knew the depths of her feelings for them. She touched his arm in a gesture of gratitude. "But it's all right. Really."

"All I'm trying to do is uphold the law, Sarah. And besides, it'll give the kids a little time to adjust to the idea of . . . leaving."

All Sarah could think about was that she'd have them with her for another day, maybe two. It might be easier on her if they just left now, but Tom was right about one thing. The kids needed a little time to get to know their father. It would be infinitely easier on them if they could do that in familiar surroundings.

Before she knew what she was doing, she'd offered her guest room to Morgan Foster, and he'd accepted.

TWO

Morgan couldn't believe the amount of food Sarah Collins laid out for supper. He could survive for two weeks on that much food. He'd done it on less. The aroma of fried chicken was enough to make his knees weak. He hadn't seen so much food at one time in years. The widow certainly didn't skimp when it came to meals. Maybe he'd misjudged her. After all, the kids seemed to adore her.

Of course, if any of his foster mothers had looked like Sarah Collins, he'd probably have worshiped the ground she walked on. At Wes's age, he'd have tried to worship a few other things, as well.

It had to cost her more than what the state paid her to buy this much food. Or so he thought, until the kids started playing their nightly game of "what isn't ours?"

The chicken was one they'd raised and butchered. Make that *chickens*—there were at least two, but the pieces were disappearing too fast to count.

The corn, beans, tomatoes, lettuce, peas, and potatoes came from the garden out back. The milk and butter came from the family cow. Who ever heard of a cow named Edna?

Even the honey for the biscuits came from beehives right there on the farm.

The only "outside" ingredients on the table according to the kids were the flour, baking soda, and salt used in the biscuits, and the oil the chicken was fried in.

So maybe he hadn't been so wrong about her in the first place. She *didn't* spend a lot of money on groceries.

And just how much work were the kids responsible for? It took a lot of effort to run a farm, even if it was only eighty acres. There was no way a woman could do it alone. No wonder she'd been eager to take in five children.

Satisfied that he'd firmed up his opinion of Sarah Collins, Morgan helped himself to some of everything on the table. After over a year of eating only what he could kill or steal, then a week of hospital mush, he had no qualms at all about taking full advantage of the widow's hospitality. Especially since he figured his own children did most of the work involved in providing the meal.

It was a shock to Sarah to sit down at dinner and see Morgan Foster at the opposite end of the table instead of the usual empty chair. Gary's chair. She tried not to look at him, but every time she looked up, her gaze collided with his.

Some women would call his eyes "bedroom

eyes.'' They were dark brown, surrounded by black lashes thick enough to make a woman jealous. Hot eyes that sent shivers of . . . something down her spine.

They were the eyes of a stranger, yet they were familiar. And they were alert to every movement around him, missing nothing as they swept across the room. Curious eyes, seeking answers to questions she didn't understand.

Hungry eyes, when he stared at all the food on the table. He seemed surprised by it somehow.

And loving eyes when he gazed on the faces of his children.

His children. It was true, they were his children, yet she loved them as if they were her own. Lord, how was she going to survive without them?

Morgan Foster was upsetting the pattern of her life. Tragedies were only supposed to happen to her every ten years. When she was ten, her mother had died of cancer. When she was twenty, her father died of a stroke. When she was thirty, her husband died of a heart attack.

According to her way of thinking, she wasn't supposed to lose anyone else until she was forty. Yet she was only thirty-two, and there sat Morgan Foster.

She blinked the moisture from her eyes and brought her mind back to the present.

''Gad, Rob, slow down,'' Connie said. ''You want Dad to think you're a pig?''

''Hey, I'm just—''

''Feeding the monster,'' Connie and Wes finished for him.

Sarah smiled at their joke. Rob's appetite was the stuff legends were made of. He either put it all in a hollow pit somewhere (the famous "monster stomach") or burned it off, for he, like his brothers, was as slim as a rail.

When she flicked her gaze over him in fondness, something odd caught her eye. She bit back a laugh and schooled her features into a semblance of severity. "Robert," she said, "I think your friend wants to be taken outside."

"Huh?" Rob asked around a mouthful of mashed potatoes. He looked surprised. She only called him Robert when he was in trouble. He swallowed. "What friend?"

Sarah pursed her lips to keep from laughing. "The one whose head is poking up out of your shirt pocket."

"Look!" Angie shrieked, pointing a stubby finger at Rob's shirt.

Connie rolled her eyes in disgust; Jeff sat across from Rob and snickered; Wes shook his head and grinned. A strangled noise came from Morgan's end of the table. All eyes focused on the slick gray head of the small snake peeking out of Rob's shirt pocket. The slender head raised farther, revealing a bright orange ring around its neck.

Rob dropped his fork with a clatter and stuffed the snake back down into hiding. When he looked up at Sarah, a guilty flush stained his cheeks. His gaze darted to his father, then back to Sarah. "Sorry," he said with a grimace. "I forgot about him." Without another word, he left the table and went outside.

While he was gone, Morgan stared at Sarah in confusion. What kind of woman would be so calm about the appearance of a snake at her dinner table? She obviously wasn't the least bit upset. She actually appeared to be fighting a grin. Her blue eyes sparkled with mirth.

A moment later Rob was back. He stopped halfway to the table, then turned back to the sink to wash his hands. "I put him in the garden," he mumbled, sliding back into his seat.

"Thank you," Sarah said. "I'm sure he'll be much happier there."

Rob cast a glance out the corner of his eye to see if his father was going to say anything, but Morgan, in an effort to keep from laughing out loud, focused his attention on his food.

The rest of the meal progressed without incident. By the time they all got up from the table, the only food left was a half-eaten dab of mashed potatoes and gravy on Angie's plate. Food that would have lasted Morgan a week had disappeared in a matter of minutes. He'd forgotten how much it took to keep a kid going.

It was something to think about. He'd never been much of a cook himself. When he and the kids got settled someplace, he'd have to hire a cook. And a housekeeper.

"Who's got KP tonight?" Connie asked.

"Sarah does," Jeff said.

"No Sarah doesn't," Sarah answered. "Sarah had KP last night."

Confident that the matter would be settled and

the kitchen would be cleaned by whosever turn it was, Sarah grabbed the bucket of green beans they'd picked earlier and escaped to the screened-in back porch to snap them.

The porch ran halfway along the east side of the house. In the late evening like this, it was cool and shaded. It was a good spot to get away from Morgan Foster. The man confused her.

With a small bucket beside her for the stems and a bowl in her lap for the edible pieces, Sarah began the boring, mindless task of snapping beans. It left her mind free to wander.

Morgan Foster was here to claim his children. She wanted to hate him for the pain she felt, but the emotion wouldn't come. He was their father, and they loved him. They belonged with him, needed him. Everyone needed a father. She could use some advice from her own father about now.

Surely the rapid pulse and difficult breathing she experienced in Morgan Foster's presence was generated by her fear of losing the children. But that didn't explain the tingling and the heat that spread from secret, long-forgotten places in her body.

The screen door creaked open. Sarah stiffened, then relaxed when she saw it was Angie. The child sat on the porch floor near Sarah's chair with Elizabeth Ann, her Cabbage Patch doll, on one knee, and Jingles, her brown teddy bear with a bell in his ear, on the other.

Sarah closed her eyes and snapped another bean, listening to the quiet conversation the child conducted with her two silent friends. Dishes clattered in the kitchen, and an argument broke out between Wes and Jeff over whether the gravy bowl should go on the top or bottom rack of the dishwasher.

Angie began singing softly, but was soon drowned out by the barking of the dogs. Sarah opened her eyes again and smiled. Connie and Rob tossed a Frisbee in the backyard, and Kermit and Miss Piggy, the German shepherds, ran their legs off trying to catch it.

Rob sailed the Frisbee over Connie's head, and Kermit saw his chance. He caught the plastic disk in midair and took off, two kids and Miss Piggy hot on his tail. The four of them circled the house twice before the kids managed to tackle Kermit and retrieve the Frisbee.

What would this place be like without the sounds of children? It was hard to remember how it was before they came. When Gary was alive, he was gone to work all day, and Sarah had been alone. But she'd never felt alone. She'd had the chickens to look after, the garden to tend, dozens of chores to keep her busy. And just knowing Gary would be home each evening, that she had someone to share her day, her life with, was comforting. No, she'd never felt alone, never been idle.

Now, when the children left, she'd have even more work. She hadn't had the horses or the cow before. Nor the dogs. And the garden was three times the size it had been. Yes, she'd have more than ever to keep her busy. But she could already feel the loneliness creeping in on her.

It was a new, alien feeling, and unwelcome.

She shoved it aside. Soon enough to give it rein after the children left. But while they were here, she intended to savor every remaining minute of their presence.

She shooed a fly away from her nose and reached for another bean to snap, surprised to find the bucket empty. She'd snapped them all.

Just then the screen door creaked again and Wes and Jeff came out, followed by their father. Morgan nodded in her direction, then his gaze traveled to Angie, where she still sat on the floor, silent now. Sarah watched his jaw harden and his eyes darken as the girl sidled up close to Sarah's leg, as if for protection. From him.

"Sun's down," Wes informed Sarah.

"Yep," Jeff said. "Chore time." Jeff, it seemed, had already loosened up in front of his dad.

But Angie was going to need a little time, and a little help. It was going to be up to Sarah to provide that help.

"Okay," she said. "Just let me set these beans in the fridge."

"Need any help?" It was Morgan's voice. For one confused instant she thought he was talking to her. Help? Carrying a bowl to the refrigerator? She glanced at him. But he wasn't talking to her, he was talking to Wes. She shook her head and carried the bowl inside.

Morgan stared at Sarah's shapely denim-clad hips until they disappeared behind the screen door. He couldn't decide which he liked better—the way the soft, worn fabric revealed those hips, or the way her T-shirt clung to and emphasized her unbound breasts. With effort, he turned back to Wes.

Wes shrugged and grinned. "Take your pick," he said.

Take my pick? For a brief second Morgan's imagination ran away with him. Then he swallowed. Oh, yeah. Chores. Help.

"Sarah takes care of the chickens and cattle, except we don't have any cattle this year, because the freezer's full."

"And I feed the ducks and geese, and look for their eggs, and help Sarah look for hen eggs," Jeff boasted.

"Connie feeds Tippy and the dogs."

"Tippy?" Morgan asked.

Just then a bell clanged near the back gate. Jeff pointed to a black-and-white Nubian goat, who wore a three-inch-long bell on a leather collar. "That's Tippy."

"Rob feeds the horses, and when they need grooming, whoever's handy helps him," Wes added.

"And what's your chore?" Morgan asked.

Wes grinned. "I milk Edna and feed the barn cats just enough to keep them hanging around so they'll catch mice."

"Don't forget Angie," Sarah said, coming back out onto the porch. "She has the most important job. She's our water girl, aren't you, sweetie?" She winked at Angie, who grinned in return.

"That's right," Angie said proudly. "I'm the water girl. Everybody needs me."

"And what does a water girl do?" Morgan asked, careful to keep his distance. He didn't want to send her running.

Shyness stole over Angie's features again when her father spoke to her. Sarah stepped up and took the girl's hand. If Angie and her father were ever going to get to know each other, Sarah figured there was no better time to give them a nudge than now. "Why don't we show your daddy what a water girl does. Okay?"

Before getting up, Angie used her free hand to carefully place Elizabeth Ann and Jingles in the chair Sarah had vacated. "Now you two sit here and wait for me," she told them softly. "I'll be back in a little bit." Then, still holding Sarah's hand, she climbed to her feet, glanced shyly at Morgan then back at Sarah. "Okay. I'm ready now."

They left the porch and headed across the backyard. Connie and Rob joined them. The German shepherds ran ahead to the gate, but Rob stood back and kept them in the yard. They whined in protest at being left behind.

Morgan looked around with interest at the place where his children had lived for two years. The garden, at the other end of the yard, was huge. At this end, set back from the yard about a hundred feet, stood a chicken house, complete with separate fenced runs along the north and south sides. The goat, cow, and horses paced restlessly in front of a three-sided loafing shed a hundred yards north of the chicken house. Off to the side was a cinder block building that could only be the wellhouse. Next sat a portable metal building. That must be the shop, or tool shed, Wes had mentioned during dinner. Next to the shop, beneath the spreading branches of a huge old elm, stood a sparkling clean riding mower and a big yellow Case tractor straight out of the fifties, complete with attached brush hog.

Thick, lush bermuda carpeted the area around the buildings, then faded out farther up the hill to the east, losing the battle to native prairie grass and clumps of love grass.

The whole place gave off a feeling of careful tending, of orderliness, and for some reason, security. Morgan had never really felt insecure in his life—at least not since reaching adulthood. But he never remembered feeling such a sense of security before, either. The place felt . . . comfortable . . . homey.

He shrugged the feeling away. This wasn't his home. They wouldn't be staying here but for a few more days.

He turned his mind back to the scene on the porch a moment ago. Gray. Sarah's eyes had been the gray of a cloudy sky. Yet this afternoon, and again at dinner, he knew they'd been blue.

It had probably just been a trick of the light. He looked up to see everyone go off in separate directions and tugged his mind back to the present. He squatted down beside Angie, careful not to get too close, while she stood next to an all-weather water faucet as tall as she was.

A few seconds later, Rob hollered from the shed, "Let 'er rip, Angie!'

With growing amazement, Morgan watched the process Angie went through. The faucet had a dual nozzle connected to it. The hose attached to one side snaked off around the corner of the chicken runs. The other side of the dual nozzle had another dual nozzle on it, with a hose extending from each opening. Each nozzle extension had a tiny drawing on it.

There was a chicken painted on the first nozzle where the hose came out. The other extension had a duck and a horse on it. The dual nozzle attached there had a duck on one side, and a horse on the other. Angie proceeded to turn all the nozzle levers so they pointed toward the horse pictures. Then she grasped the big handle on the faucet with both hands and pushed it up over her head with a grunt. Morgan clenched his fists in an effort to keep from helping her. When she finally got it all the way up, he relaxed. The pipe gurgled, a hose jumped along the ground, and a moment later water gushed out of the hose Rob held over at the shed.

"See?" Angie said, squinting up at him. "It's easy."

"I need water!" Jeff called. He was in the last chicken run, and was surrounded not by chickens, but by baby mallards, and one worried, fussy mama mallard, whose quack sounded like startled, raucous laughter. Angie turned the appropriate levers so Rob could fill the small plastic wading pool inside the pen.

The whole operation was smooth and flawless, and all the kids seemed to be enjoying themselves. They didn't realize just how much work they were accomplishing.

When everyone was finished with the water, Angie reached up and grabbed the faucet handle with both hands again. This time she hung on and lifted her feet off the ground. The handle came slowly down to its resting place. One hose gave a final jerk, and Morgan heard water being sucked back down the tall pipe until it was empty.

It was a neat operation. But he wondered why Sarah didn't just put in another faucet out at the shed. She surely couldn't leave the hoses strung out everywhere in the winter; they'd freeze and break. That meant hauling water, probably in buckets. A second faucet made much more sense to him than the current arrangement.

A few minutes later, everyone gathered at Angie's faucet, Wes carrying a bucket of milk, Sarah a basket of big, brown eggs. As they walked back to the house, they all began hollering out their "good nights" to the animals.

"Good night, chickies!"

" 'Night, Edna!"

" 'Night, horsies!"

" 'Night, duckies!"

" 'Night, goosies!"

" 'Night, kitties!"

Then, in unison, "Good night, John Boy!"

Morgan smiled at their play. God, he'd never seen his kids so happy and playful before. Not that they'd ever really been unhappy, he supposed. But Joyce had run a quiet, controlled house. No muss, no fuss, no noise. Everything in its proper place. Including the children. And him.

Sarah Collins, however, was not Joyce. Her house, her entire farm, in fact, seemed neat and orderly. But it was a boisterous, fun-filled order. One that kids thrived on.

Feelings of doubt and inadequacy swept over him. Would he be able to provide such a healthy environment for them as this? One they would come to love as much as they obviously loved this place?

And what about their feelings for Sarah Collins? What was he going to do about that?

For that matter, he wondered about his own feelings for Sarah Collins. He'd come here prepared to hate her, to save his children from some terrible existence. But when he looked into those big blue eyes of hers—or were they gray?—something happened inside him. Something unexpected. Something he had no business feeling at all.

Sarah tiptoed past Morgan Foster's room and headed quietly upstairs to check on the children. They'd been in bed for a couple of hours now, and she always checked on them before she went to bed herself. She wasn't about to stop just because their father had decided to show up.

She gazed longingly, lovingly, at each precious face and placed a tender kiss on each beloved brow. It was a good thing Wes and Rob were asleep or they wouldn't have allowed such a thing.

They had decided long ago they were much too old for motherly kisses.

She lingered over each rumpled bed. A dull pain stabbed at her heart. How many more nights would she be able to check on them, tuck them in, kiss them good night? One? Two?

Please, God, don't let him take them yet.

When she went back downstairs a few minutes later, she noticed the door to Morgan's room standing open. She found him in the kitchen getting a glass of milk. Funny, he didn't look like the milk type.

"I hope you don't mind," he said, raising his glass to her. "But this is the best milk I've ever had. As a matter of fact, it's the first milk I've had in years."

Sarah tried to smile. "Of course not. Help yourself whenever you want."

Morgan drained his glass and turned to rinse it out. Sarah gasped. The back of his beige sweater was covered with a wide streak of dried blood, and looked like it was stuck to his skin. "What happened to you?"

He turned, his look saying, "What are you talking about?"

"Your back."

"What about my back?"

Sarah placed her hands on her hips and gave him a terse look. "For one thing, it's covered in blood. For another, I strongly suspect that when you pull off that sweater, you're going to take a great deal of skin with it."

Morgan looked puzzled. He twisted his head to see his back reflected in the window over the sink. "Oh, that. It's nothing. A little souvenir from my trip home."

"Nice places you visit, Foster. Come on." She grabbed him by the wrist and led him back toward his room. "Let's see if we can get that sweater off without removing your hide."

Morgan followed docilely. "I've had women want to get my clothes off before, but they never used quite that tone of voice."

Sarah stopped, turned her head, and looked him up and down . . . slowly. "I'll bet."

Good Lord, what was she doing? She was flirting with him! She couldn't remember the last time she'd flirted with a man. And this was one man she didn't intend to mess with at all. What in the world would he think of her!

"We'll soak it loose," she said. A few minutes later she had him facedown on the bed, towels under and around him, and a warm, wet towel laying across the back of his sweater.

She repeatedly dipped the towel in a bucket of warm water, then pressed it against the dried blood, trying to soften it so she could get his sweater off without removing his skin, too.

"I'd like to thank you for what you've done for my kids," he said softly.

Sarah's hands stilled for a moment. "You're welcome, but your thanks aren't necessary. Just having them in my home has been thanks enough. They're very . . . special to me."

"I can see that."

"They never gave up on you, you know," she offered. "Not for a minute. All of them, even Angie, who never knew you, believed that one day you'd come for them. They love you very much."

"All but Angie," he said, a note of sadness in his voice. "I didn't even know she existed until yesterday."

From things Wes had told her, she'd figured as much. "Just give her a little time. She's been through a lot for one so young. First she lost her mother and stepfather, then Gary."

"Who's Gary?"

"He was my husband. When the children first came here Angie wouldn't have much to do with me, but she adored Gary, and he her. Three months later he died. She took it pretty hard."

Morgan snorted. "And you didn't?"

Sarah stiffened. "Another remark like that, and I'll forget about soaking this sweater loose; I'll rip it off for you."

"Take it easy," he said into the pillow. "I only meant—"

"I don't care what you meant, Mr. Foster. I loved my husband very much, for your information. But I wasn't talking about me, I was talking about Angie."

"Don't you think you could call me Morgan? Mr. Foster sounds a bit stuffy, seeing as how we're sharing a bed at the moment."

Sarah tried to work up a good, healthy rage at his suggestive comment, but failed. Instead, she laughed. "I guess we are, at that. What would the children think?"

"I don't know what the others would say," he answered, his voice turning serious. "But I've seen the way Wes looks at you. He'd probably be jealous as hell."

Sarah dropped the wet, blood-smeared towel into the bucket with a splash. "You're crazy!"

"Am I?" He peered up at her with one eye. "I remember what it was like to be fifteen. I can't really say I blame him. If one of my foster mothers had looked like you, I'd probably still be living with her."

"You lived in a foster home?"

"Several," he said tersely. "My oldest son's got the hots for you, Mrs. Collins."

"That's the most outrageous thing I've ever heard!"

"It's the truth, though."

"It's the end of this discussion, is what it is," she said firmly. "Sit up. Your sweater's loose now." The very idea of him thinking Wes had a crush on her. How absurd. How disgusting.

As Morgan sat up, the creaking of the mattress filled the stiff silence. She eased the sweater up over his back, and he pulled it off. In addition to the ugly cut that ran from his left shoulder, across his back, halfway to his right hip, there was a bloody, once-white bandage taped several inches beneath his right arm.

She left the stained bandage alone while she cleaned the larger gash. Her fingers trailed the length of the wound, feeling for any feverish spots. The only heat she detected was in her own cheeks a moment later when she realized her hand had strayed to stroke the smooth, firm skin of his back. Beneath her palm, his muscles tensed.

Good Lord, what was she doing? She jerked her hand away and glared at his broad, tanned back, somehow managing to blame Morgan Foster for her own lack of sense.

Get to work, Sarah.

She smeared a mixture of vitamin E and garlic oil into the cut, all the time wondering about where he'd been, what he'd been doing for four years that kept him away from his children. His muscles were rock-hard and bulging, but underneath, he was thin. A little too thin for a man his size. He hadn't been eating much lately, that was her guess.

She peeled off the bandage on his side, being careful not to pull the skin. The wound didn't look infected, but it still oozed red. "When did this happen?" she asked, concern in her voice.

"A couple of weeks ago."

"Weeks! These should have scabbed over days ago. What have you been doing to them? Why haven't you seen a doctor?"

"Seen a doctor? I've spent the entire week I've been back in the States flat on my back in the hospital. I guarantee you, I've seen plenty of doctors."

Sarah shuddered to think what kind of shape the wounds had been in if they looked this bad after a week in the hospital. "I'd find myself a new doctor if I were you."

She covered both wounds with gauze bandages,

then said, "Don't put a shirt on in the morning till I've had a chance to check these again."

Morgan sat up and looked at her, his eyes boring into hers. "Thank you. You're a nice person, Sarah Collins."

Sarah snorted; there was no other way to describe the sound she made. With quick, angry jerks, she collected her towels and bucket.

"I'm not nice, I'm a fool," she said with disgust.

"Why's that?"

"Any woman in her right mind would hate you for showing up here after all this time to take the kids away."

"And you don't hate me?"

She stood before him, tense, confused. "I want to, but I can't. At least not yet. Maybe when you go I will. I love your children, Morgan. I love them like they were my own. In my mind and in my heart, they're mine. I can't have children of my own. Yours filled an empty spot in me I didn't even know existed.

"I'm not saying any of this to make you feel sorry for me. Pity is the last thing I want. I just want you to understand how I feel. You're their father. They love you, and they need you. They've waited a long time for you to come home."

Sarah took a deep breath and blinked the moisture from her eyes. "I want what's best for them. If you're planning on making a home for them and staying with them, instead of gallivanting all over the world, then I'm glad, for their sakes, that you came. I'll miss them terribly. But you're their father; they belong with you."

She turned and left him there, quiet tears slipping down her face.

Morgan stared at the empty doorway and listened to her soft footsteps receding through the house. A thoughtful frown marred his face. There wasn't a doubt in his mind that she'd meant every word she said.

The lady certainly has class.

And her eyes were gray. Definitely gray.

Sarah lay in bed for hours staring at the reflection of the outdoor utility light on the ceiling.

Okay, she told herself. *So I'm attracted to him.* So what? The last man she'd been attracted to was Gary. That was the right time, the right place. This wasn't. Morgan Foster was only here for a few days. Just long enough to regain custody of his children. Then he'd be gone. And so would they.

Okay. So it hurt. It wasn't the first thing in her life that hurt, and it wouldn't be the last.

What did she care if he had the most touchable skin in the world? And the most beautiful male chest. She'd never seen a grown man with a hairless chest before. It was smooth and tanned, the muscles forming hills and valleys that invited a woman's fingers to explore.

But not her fingers. No, not hers.

In spite of a nearly sleepless night, Sarah woke at her usual time, sunup, without benefit of an alarm. Her first thoughts were of the man in her guest room. What would his back look like this morning?

She put the coffee on, then went out early to let the chickens loose for the day. She'd wait to check on Morgan until after the kids came downstairs. He'd be awake for sure by then. There was no way he'd be able to sleep through their racket.

As soon as the kids were outside tending to their morning chores, which were few, Sarah knocked on Morgan's door. It opened a second later, and she was disconcerted to see he'd done as she'd asked. He'd left his shirt off.

She didn't know where to look. His broad, bare chest did strange things to her breathing. His deep-brown eyes weren't any safer.

"Good morning," he murmured.

When she entered his room he shut the door. She started to object, but he said, "I'd rather the kids didn't see my back just yet."

Sarah nodded her understanding. No sense upsetting them. "Turn around, and I'll check those bandages."

He did as she asked. When she removed the tape and gauze she was pleased to see the wounds much improved. "I'd like to leave the bandages off and let some air get to these," she said. She handed him the T-shirt she had draped over her shoulder. "If you wear this, you won't ruin any of your shirts, and I think it'll be loose enough to let the air circulate beneath it."

Morgan held the huge T-shirt up and grimaced. The thing would obviously swallow him. "Your husband's?"

Sarah laughed. "Heavens no! Gary wasn't even as large as you are. That was my father's."

"Was?"

"He died over twelve years ago."

"You've kept his T-shirts all this time?"

Sarah simply shrugged, not daring to tell him why. She made what felt suspiciously like an escape as quickly as possible.

It didn't do her any good in the long run. When they all sat down to breakfast forty-five minutes later, Angie got everyone's attention by pointing at her father and demanding, "Why's he wearing your nightgown, Sarah?"

Sarah's cheeks burned with fire.

Morgan nearly choked on a mouthful of coffee.

THREE

Sarah's day went downhill from there. She escaped to the garden immediately after breakfast. She couldn't decide whether she wanted to stuff the weeds she was pulling into Angie's big mouth, fling them in Morgan Foster's face, or crawl into one of the small holes left where the roots came out of the ground.

Every time she looked up, Morgan was somewhere near, watching her, a speculative gleam in his eye. He'd grin slightly and glance down at the T-shirt he wore, then at her. Then he'd rub the T-shirt across his chest with the flat of his palm, slowly, and his grin would widen. That grin did funny things to her heartbeat.

He did it several times that morning, and each time he did, she felt like screaming. When he entered the garden and strolled toward her, she pretended great interest in a row of onions. She was saved from having to deal with him when Jeff and Rob came barreling up to the fence.

"Can we invite Ben and Kenny over so they can

meet Dad?" Rob asked. He and Jeff looked from Sarah to Morgan, not quite sure which one they should be asking.

Sarah didn't hesitate. They might be Morgan's children, but this was still her home. She didn't want him to get the idea she was going to start deferring to him on who could come over. "Sure. Give them a call."

"Great!" Jeff hollered. The two boys bounded into the house with a banging of the screen door.

"Who are Ben and Kenny?" Morgan asked, turning his gaze from the house to Sarah.

"They live behind us, over the hill. They're Rob and Jeff's best friends. Their father, Barry, is a farmer, and Rita, their mother, has been my best friend since high school."

Morgan smirked and cocked a brow while rubbing his hand across his chest. "Does your best friend know you loan your nightgowns out to men you've barely met? Not many women would give the shirt off their back to a stranger."

"Oh?" she said, feigning confusion. "They don't? Funny. I do it all the time."

"I'd watch out if I were you, Dad," Wes said, joining them quietly, startling Sarah. "The next time you need to borrow her nightgown, she might lend you that little pink lace thing she's got. You'd look pretty silly in it."

The teasing glint faded from Morgan's eyes. "Pink lace?"

Sarah fumed at his tone and his look. She knew exactly what he was thinking, after that comment he made last night about Wes. He thought she'd been parading herself around in scanty night clothes in front of his impressionable teenage son. She opened her mouth to set him straight, then clamped it shut. Her chin set in lines of pure mutiny and stubbornness. Let him think whatever he wanted. She didn't owe him any explanations. He wouldn't be around long enough to worry about, anyway, she thought with a pang.

"Come on, Dad," Wes said, unaware of what was going on. "I'll show you around the place."

Sarah watched them go and fumed silently. Enough of this weeding by hand. She felt like clobbering something. She grabbed the hoe and took her anger out on the weeds that dared to flourish in the walkways between her vegetable-growing beds.

Rob and Jeff exploded out the back door of the house and ran past Sarah without a glance. They zigzagged their way up the back hill, obviously headed to meet Ben and Kenny.

Breathing heavily a few minutes later, Sarah leaned on her hoe and glanced down the walkway. She should get angry in the garden more often, she thought. She'd weeded that path in less than half her usual time.

"Where do you want to start, Dad?" Wes asked once they were clear of the garden.

"Why don't we start with that pink lace nightgown?"

Wes's head snapped around at Morgan's grim tone. His brows lowered in confusion. "What do you mean?"

"I mean, does Sarah Collins make it a habit to prance around in skimpy pink lace in front of teenage boys?"

Wes's eyes widened in amazement. "Of course not! And it wasn't skimpy." When Morgan simply looked at him, Wes frowned. "Gary bought her this pink nightgown right after we came here to live. He asked her to model it for him, and she did. That's all there was to it."

Morgan could tell by the fire in his son's eyes that he'd struck a nerve. "That must have been nearly two years ago. It must have made a hell of an impression on you for you to remember it all this time."

"As a matter of fact, it did," Wes claimed, sounding defensive. "It was the only time I ever saw Sarah dressed in something Mom would have worn. It didn't suit her. She even said it itched. Why are you making such a big deal out of it, anyway?"

Morgan ignored the question. "You like her a lot, don't you." He didn't ask; he said it as though it were fact.

"Sure I do," Wes said, relaxing. "You will, too, once you get to know her. She's the neatest lady I've ever met, Dad."

Morgan stopped to wipe a glob of chicken manure off his shoe. "How so?"

Wes shrugged and led his father away from the buildings. "I don't know. I guess it's because she treats me, all of us really, like equals. She doesn't talk down to us like most adults do. When we need mothering, she mothers us. When we make her mad, she lets us know. The rest of the time, she's our friend. She's the best friend I've ever had.''

Morgan frowned. Getting Wes to admit that he more than liked Sarah wasn't going to be easy. And on the outside chance that Wes didn't understand his own feelings, Morgan decided it might be best not to push just yet. He let it drop.

Wes took him everywhere. The land on Sarah's farm was not smooth and flat, not particularly suited to growing crops, but cattle and horses would thrive on it. He saw the pond where the geese and ducks lived. Then there were the fishing ponds. One for bass, one for crappie, and one for catfish.

''Do you ever swim in them?'' Morgan asked.

Wes grinned. ''Not on your life. We're not too fond of snakes and snapping turtles.''

To the south there was a persimmon grove. Wes said several deer hung around there in the fall. Toward the north was a stretch of about twenty acres of natural woods with a creek flowing across one end of it. The rest of the land was rough pasture, split by washouts here and there. The back of the property was somewhere over the east hill, beyond the catfish pond.

On the way back toward the house, Wes stopped and introduced Morgan to the horses. ''This is Spot,'' he said, patting a black-and-white Appaloosa on the neck.

Morgan's lips twitched. ''Spot?''

''Well, that's not her real name, but that's what Angie calls her. She's Sarah and Angie's horse.

The twins have the roan. They call him The Fonz. And Black belongs to Jeff and me."

"Belongs?" Morgan said, his tone skeptical.

"Yeah. It was the neatest thing. We never did figure out how Sarah got them here and into the shed without us seeing them. We just got up Christmas morning, that first Christmas we were here, and saw these packages under the tree. One for me and Jeff, one for the twins, and one addressed to Angie and Sarah. They were bridles. We didn't know what to think until Sarah took us outside. Wow! Were we ever surprised."

"You mean Sarah bought these horses just for you kids?"

"Yep. The dogs, too. And the cow," he added, his mouth twisting up at one corner."

Morgan answered the grin. "She thought you wanted a cow?"

"She wanted to make sure we always had plenty of milk. It was a good thing, too. Edna gives about two gallons a day, and we drink every drop of it."

Morgan was quiet the rest of the way back to the house. So Sarah had bought horses, dogs, and a cow, just because of his kids. How the hell could she afford that? Even with growing their own food, the small amount she received from the state each month wouldn't keep five kids in blue jeans. Then there was the feed for all those animals.

His thoughts were interrupted by the actions of his youngest daughter. Angie was crawling on all fours past the chicken pens, heedless of any moist globs in her path. "Go! Go!" she shouted, urging a four-inch round turtle along the ground.

She looked up and saw Wes and Morgan. Her big brown eyes skittered away from Morgan and settled on her brother. "I found him, Wessy! This is the one. I'm gonna name him Speedy. Think he'll win?"

Wes's face filled with affection for his little sister. "He sure looks like a fast one. Where you gonna keep him till the race?"

Angie scrunched up her face and bit her bottom lip, her eyes darting all around. Then she grinned. "There!" She pointed to an unused chicken run on the south side of the chicken house, one of the "winter" runs, as Wes had earlier described them. Angie grabbed up her turtle with both hands and carried him into the pen.

Morgan tried to picture Joyce allowing a daughter of hers—or a son, for that matter—to get within ten feet of a turtle (outside of the zoo, of course), much less touch one. He nearly laughed aloud at the sheer horror and disgust that would have contorted Joyce's face if such a thing would have happened.

"He needs water," Wes reminded Angie.

"I'm gonna do like Jeffy did last year. I'm gonna dig a hole and put a pan in it. That way he can crawl right in and go swimming anytime he wants."

"What will you feed him?"

Angie thought a minute, then grinned. "We'll go to the feed store and get some Purina Turtle Chow."

Morgan pursed his lips to keep from laughing, but Wes didn't hold back. "You'd better think of something else, kid. I don't think Purina makes Turtle Chow."

"How come?" she demanded, her little brow puckering in a frown. "Kenny says they make Hog Chow, and you said they make Catfish Chow, and they have Horse Chow and Dog Chow and Cat Chow. How come they don't have Turtle Chow?"

Wes shrugged in surrender. "Maybe they do. We'll find out."

Morgan and Wes walked away as Angie started digging her hole in the ground with an old rusty garden trowel. Morgan frowned. The only time Angie had looked at him had been once, quickly, out of the corner of her eye. She'd talked to Wes, and even the turtle, but not to him.

"What's this turtle race she's talking about?"

"It's the Fourth of July thing they have up at Chandler every year. They have horseshoe pitching, dancing, lots of food, that kind of stuff."

"And turtle races?"

"Yeah," Wes said with a grin. "We watched them last year, and Sarah promised Angie and Jeff they could enter this year if they wanted. Jeff's been talking about it for weeks."

Morgan's frown deepened. July Fourth was more than a week away. He'd surely have his custody papers by then. He didn't want to hang around here any longer than necessary.

Once again his thoughts were interrupted when Jeff and Rob sprinted around the corner of the house, followed by two blond-haired, freckle-faced, blue-eyed boys, one around twelve, the other about nine, he guessed.

Rob and Jeff introduced them as Ken and Benny Hudspeth, their "very best friends."

Morgan sighed and frowned. Sarah, horses, dogs, turtle races, and now, best friends. How were his children going to deal with leaving it all behind?

Late-evening shadows stretched from the back of the house as the sun sank lower in the west. The stiff, hot wind had settled into a warm, soft breeze, and Sarah and Morgan sat on the back porch drinking iced tea and watching the kids at their various play.

Sarah screwed up her courage and asked the question uppermost in her mind. "Will you be leaving as soon as you get the custody papers?"

Morgan set down his tea glass and kept his eyes trained on Angie in the swing. "Actually, I'm glad you asked that. It seems there's a turtle race coming up at the end of next week. I was wondering if you'd mind if we stayed till then. I'd be willing to make it worth your while."

Sarah had begun to relax at his words. He wasn't in a hurry to leave. The implications of his last statement, however, caused her muscles to tense. "Worth my while?" she asked softly, slowly.

If Morgan had known her better, he would have recognized that tone and retracted his last statement. But he didn't, so he plunged on. "Room and board, that sort of thing. It must have cost you a small fortune to keep the kids for this long. When we leave I'd like to settle up with you, so be figuring what I owe for all their clothes and things, as well as for the horses and dogs, and their keep."

He watched as Sarah's hand clenched around her glass until her fingers turned white. She took so long to answer that he wondered if she'd heard him. "Sarah?"

"I'm not after your money, Mr. Foster."

So, we're back to Mr. Foster again, are we? What the hell's the matter with her, anyway?

"I never said you were, Sarah." He used her name deliberately, but failed to get a response out of her. "I'd just like to repay you for what you've spent on my children. I can't even imagine how you've been able to afford them this long."

"How and what I can afford is none of your business," she said between clenched teeth. "I thank you for your offer, but it isn't necessary. And you can't buy the horses and dogs from me because they aren't mine. They belong to your children. If they can't take them with them wherever you're planning to go, I'll keep them here until they tell me they don't want them anymore."

"You're angry, and I don't understand why."

"Why?" she asked, finally turning to look at him, eyes the color of gathering thunderheads. "I'll tell you why, Mr. Foster. I don't take money for something I did out of love. I greatly resent your implying that I would."

"I get it," he said, a slow grin spreading across his face. "You're still mad because I found out I'm wearing your nightgown, right?"

Sarah jumped to her feet and whirled toward the

door. "This has nothing to do with that. For some kind of government secret agent, you aren't very bright, are you? No wonder this country's in such sad shape."

She yanked open the kitchen door, then did what he'd heard her scold the children for doing—she slammed it behind her.

Morgan stared at the closed door, heard the echo of her exit ring in his ears, and blinked slowly. What the hell was the matter with that woman, anyway?

After the kids were in bed, Sarah slipped out to the front porch and sat in her mother's swing. The air was body temperature and heavy with moisture. Cicadas buzzed in the trees, and June bugs whacked against the window screen, trying to get to the light on the other side.

Kermit and Miss Piggy came wagging their tails and trying to lick her in the face. "Cut it out, you two. I didn't come out here to get slobbered on." The words that could have sent the two off with tails tucked and ears flat were softened by a giggle.

Another June bug hit the window screen and both dogs took off in pursuit. June bugs were a doggy delicacy.

Sarah sent the swing into motion with a push of her toe against the porch. The familiar creak of old wood and dry chain soothed the restlessness that had plagued her all day.

One of the most precious memories of her childhood was of her mother on this very swing on a bright spring morning, with a bouquet of wildflowers held gently in her work-worn hands. It was just about the only memory of her mother she had left. All the others, just like the wildflowers, had faded with time.

A puff of wind brought the fragrance of the honeysuckle that bloomed at the corner of the house. She inhaled deeply and smiled.

The storm door creaked open and Morgan stepped out. Sarah's smile faded. Every time she saw him she was reminded that he would soon take the children and go. She'd be alone then. Totally, completely alone for the first time in her life. Briefly she allowed the thought to terrify her before reminding herself that as long as she had the farm, she'd never be alone.

"What are you going to do with this place all to yourself once we're gone?" Morgan asked. Had he been reading her thoughts? He sat down next to her uninvited and unwelcome.

"Not that it's any of your business, but I believe I'll manage."

He spread his knees wide. His thigh brushed against hers every time the swing moved forward. The touch sent sparks shooting to her abdomen, and she couldn't truthfully blame her difficulty breathing entirely on the humidity.

He turned his shadowed face toward hers. The night closed in, surrounding them in intimacy, creating a secluded island there on the old swing. He leaned slightly toward her. Her gaze focused on his full lips. Was he going to kiss her?

"Did you ever think of selling the place?"

Sarah's eyes popped open wide. She refused to

acknowledge the acute disappointment crushing down on her. Foolish disappointment. "Why would I want to do that?"

Morgan shrugged, disrupting the rhythm of the swing the same way he was disrupting the rhythm of her life. "It's an awful lot of work for one person; an awful lot of room for one person."

"I'll try not to overdo or get lost."

"Don't get defensive on me. I just thought I'd bring it up. It's a great place for kids, and my kids sure seem to love it here. If you were interested in selling, I wouldn't have to uproot them again. I'd make you a fair offer."

Sarah sat perfectly still, not even breathing, while she counted to ten. Twice. "Let me explain something to you, Mr. Foster."

"Are we back to that again?"

"This farm is not just any old piece of real estate up for grabs by whoever wants it. My grandparents built this place from nothing, *with* nothing but their bare hands and a team of mules. They worked side by side and raised their family here. They died here. My mother was born in this house. She and my father both died here. *I* was born in this house. And God willing, I'll live here until I die. If that doesn't give you your answer, then I'll get real plain. The answer is no. And don't ever ask again."

The swing jerked and shuddered when she stood. Morgan halfway expected the front door to slam shut behind her when she went in the house. Slam shut and lock, to keep him out. But it didn't. She caught the storm door behind her and closed it with a soft click.

Well, he'd sure put his foot in it that time. He'd had no idea she felt so strongly about her farm. She was a single woman who would soon be living alone. He couldn't imagine any woman he knew choosing to live so far from a town.

Correction. City. The women he knew lived in big, sprawling, bustling cities.

Sarah Collins was entirely outside his realm of experience.

Morgan drove into Oklahoma City the next day, bought himself a family-size station wagon, and returned his rental car. Afterward, he went to Tom Cartwright's office. The custody papers were ready and waiting for him. On the way back to Sarah's, he decided to open a new bank account and have Benson forward his back pay to him in Oklahoma. Morgan had already passed through the town of Meeker, so instead of turning off on the road to the farm, he stayed on the highway until he reached Prague, the next town, about five miles beyond Sarah's road.

He stopped at the first bank he came to, went inside, and located the New Accounts desk, where he told the woman what he needed. She took down his name then asked for his address. The only one he had was Sarah's, so he gave it. The middle-aged woman behind the desk frowned through her bifocals and studied what she'd just written. A moment later a huge smile came over her face.

"You must be the father of Sarah's children," she cried.

Morgan felt a guilty flush stain his cheeks. He'd been thinking about Sarah most of the day. If his thoughts weren't exactly about fathering children, they were damn close. He cleared his throat and tried to smile. "Something like that," he said.

"Well, it sure is nice to meet you. I'm Mrs. Selznik. I'll bet those kids of yours were sure excited to see you. You must be mighty proud of them."

Morgan was at a loss. He hadn't lived in or near a small town since his childhood. He'd forgotten how much everyone knew about everyone else's business.

"I must say," the woman rattled on, "all your children certainly favor their father. Why, they're the spittin' image of you."

Several people must have overheard, for they turned to look him over. Morgan felt like sliding under his chair. Who were these people, anyway? A sudden longing for big-city anonymity seized him. He finished his business at the bank as rapidly as possible.

When he returned to the farm, Morgan stood looking out the back door, sipping iced tea and playing with the change in his pocket. He wasn't used to being idle. Everyone had something to do but him. Rob and Jeff had gone to the Hudspeths' to play, Wes and Connie had taken the horses for a ride, and Angie was upstairs taking a nap.

The Widow Collins, too, was busy, as usual. The woman never sat still. She was out in the garden again on her hands and knees, with that cute little rear end of hers wrapped in skintight faded denim pointed in his direction.

The hand in his pocket wrapped itself around a handful of change and pressed the coins into his suddenly damp palm. A moment later he jerked his hand from his pocket and spun away from the door. He needed something to do, something physical, something sweaty. He somehow doubted the Widow Collins would go along with the type of physical, sweaty exercise that came to mind when he looked at her cute little rear.

Sarah Collins wasn't his type of woman, anyway. He'd always been drawn more to sophisticated, somewhat cool socialites, like Joyce. Not wholesome, down-to-earth outdoors types. At least, not until now.

He definitely needed something to do.

An hour later, Morgan peeled off his shirt and used it to wipe the sweat from his face. He'd found something to do. He'd been looking for Wes when he rounded the corner of the loafing shed and noticed the nearby plum tree was using its limbs to pry loose a corner of the shed's roof. One limb had already grown more than a foot inside the building.

He'd lopped off the offending branches, then gone to work repairing the roof. He stood back now, the hot wind cool against the sweat pouring down his chest, and surveyed his work. With the kind of work he usually did, he rarely, if ever, got to see the results of a job successfully completed. It felt good to be able to do so now.

From the kitchen window Sarah watched the sweat glisten on the rippling muscles across Morgan's nearly healed back. She dug her nails into the potato she'd just peeled and felt her knees turn to jelly. Lord, what a body. Broad shoulders tapered to narrow waist and hips, then flowed smoothly into long, muscular legs. Her fingers tingled with the thought of wiping all that sweat from his back.

The banging of the screen door on the porch interrupted her fantasy, and she was grateful. There was no point to it. She gave a vicious swipe with the potato peeler, then stared in amazement as the tips of her fingernails dropped into the sink along with a thick slice of potato.

With a muttered curse, she dropped the already-peeled potato into the pan and rinsed her hands. Her eyes widened. She could have sworn she'd peeled enough potatoes to feed an army. Instead, the lone potato in the pan stared back at her. It had a curve slashed into it, like a smile. The stupid spud was laughing at her. With a growl at her own idiocy, she set to work again and tried to keep her mind off the man who was ruining her life.

She'd seen him prune back the plum tree and fix that corner of the roof. Afterward, her gaze followed him as he found a can of WD-40 and sprayed the sticky latch on the gate. Then he replaced two split boards on the stall inside the shed. They were all things she'd been putting off doing for months. Years, in the case of the roof corner.

Because of his job in the city, Gary never had much time to help with repairs, so Sarah did the most crucial things first, and let the others slide until she had more time. But since the kids came, there never seemed to be enough time.

As she peeled more potatoes she acknowledged, not for the first time, that she preferred spending time doing things with and for the children. Other things could wait.

Now Morgan was taking up the slack. During the next few days he slipped into life on Sarah's farm as though he'd been born to it. Once in a while she and Morgan even worked together, but not often.

Usually it was Morgan and Wes. Gradually, all the children came to accept him, Angie being the exception. She still wasn't sure about having a father. But Sarah knew if anyone could win her over, it would be Morgan. He was very good at fathering.

Besides . . . any man who could produce such beautiful, wonderful children couldn't be all bad, could he?

Three nights later Morgan lay in bed, wide awake like he'd been every night lately, and stared at the flashes of lightning dancing across the ceiling. Thunder rumbled in the distance, and the soft patter of rain should have relaxed him. It didn't.

The physical labor wasn't helping. He was still wound up tighter than a watch spring. His muscles quivered with nervous energy, even though he'd done the work of three men during the past few days.

And it was all because of the woman sleeping on the other side of the house.

While they each went about their separate labors during the day, Sarah Collins was never out of his thoughts. Every time he looked her way, it was as if she felt it, and those soft quizzical gray eyes sought and found his. Each time it happened, he found it increasingly difficult to look away.

Something pulled him toward her, and he fought it as hard as he'd fought for his life in the Central American jungles. Maybe what attracted him was the way those worn denims hugged her hips, or the way her soft T-shirts clung to her breasts. That was part of it, he knew. But there was something more, something he couldn't name.

He knew she felt it, too, at least the physical part. Why else would she have started wearing a bra two days ago, for the first time since he'd been here? If she thought that little scrap of fabric would keep him from staring, she was mistaken.

She kept an emotional distance between them, but that didn't stop him from filling his eyes with her.

It took a certain, special woman to take in five homeless children. And she'd kept them, despite the loss of her husband. While going through that traumatic experience, perhaps she'd needed the children as much as they had needed her.

But she'd done so much more than simply keep them. She'd coddled them, loved them, nurtured them over the death of their mother. If somebody gave an award for the happiest, most well-adjusted children on earth, he figured his would win. And the credit would all belong to Sarah Collins.

He was more grateful to her than he knew how

to express. He owed her more than he could ever repay. But gratitude, simple or otherwise, didn't explain the feelings he had for her.

Every day he witnessed her warmth, attention, and love being showered freely on his children. He felt an aching need to be a recipient of her bounty. What was it like to be the center of someone's world? Sarah's world? He found himself wanting desperately to know.

A sound intruded on his musings. It took him a second to identify it as the frantic squawking of a chicken. With a start, he realized chickens needed a good reason to squawk at night. Before he could even swing his legs to the floor, the dogs started barking.

He fumbled in the dark for his jeans, and by the time he'd pulled them up and stepped into his shoes, he heard a crash. His spine tingled. Someone was in the living room. Then he heard a muttered curse and recognized Sarah's voice.

When he got to the living room it was empty. By the light from the kitchen, he saw the glass door of the usually locked gun cabinet swing closed. An empty space in the middle of the rack told him a rifle was missing. He stepped into the kitchen in time to see Sarah dashing out the back door.

While he wondered what the devil was going on, he noticed she wore one of those huge T-shirts like she'd given him. Except for her boots, that appeared to be all she had on. As he followed, she dashed off the porch and into the rain, a rifle in one hand and a flashlight in the other.

Sarah, her ears tuned to the chickens' squawking, didn't hear Morgan follow her from the house. She dashed through the light rain, across the yard, and out the back gate. At the chicken house, she shoved open the screen door and flipped the light switch. The noise of squawking birds and flapping wings was deafening. Feathers and feed and dust flew everywhere, but there was no sign of whoever, or whatever, was causing all the excitement. She paused a second and wiped the rain from her face with the hand that held the flashlight.

Then a louder, more frantic squawking came from outside in one of the runs. She spun on one heel toward the door and ran smack into something solid. Her heart jumped to her throat, blocking the scream that tried to get out. Her eyes focused on Morgan's face just as his large, hard hands grasped her shoulders.

"What is it?"

In that instant she had to force herself to remember the problem outside rather than the smooth, bare chest before her. "Outside," she said with a gasp.

Outside, she shined the flashlight's wide beam into the first run. Nothing. But in the second run, Easter, the big colorful rooster Connie had named for the day he hatched, beat the air with frantic wings and screeched at the top of his lungs. A possum had him by the tail feathers.

Sarah swung open the gate, then had to catch it as it sagged. That answered the question of how the possum got in the pen. The bottom hinge was broken. One of the horses probably kicked the old rusted thing.

The possum didn't appear to be a bit intimidated by the beam of light or the two humans behind it. Sarah shouted at the animal and nudged it with her rifle. The dumb thing didn't even blink, just held on to its future dinner.

"Over my dead body," Sarah muttered. "Here." She slammed the flashlight into Morgan's stomach, then used the rifle barrel to pry the possum loose. If she shot him now, she'd probably kill poor Easter, too.

The possum finally let loose, a few colorful tail feathers poking out of its mouth, and waddled over into the corner. Sarah scooped Easter up in one arm and kept the rifle pointed at the possum. She tossed Easter through the small door to the inside pen. The rooster danced and screeched and flapped his wings. Not smart enough to be afraid once the possum no longer had a hold on him, he tried to get back out the door. Sarah shut it in his face.

"Stand back," she said to Morgan while her eyes remained on the possum. "I want him out of here." She had to prod the possum with the barrel of her gun. "March, you lousy chicken-eater."

Morgan kept the flashlight trained on the creature, and when she had the possum several feet away from the run, she raised the rifle to her shoulder and took aim. Damn, but she hated to kill animals. Even ones who were trying to eat her chickens. Why couldn't the fool things just stay out in the woods and eat mice and rats, for crying out loud?

Morgan must have realized her reluctance. He

took the gun from her hands and passed her the flashlight. "You want it dead, or just gone?"

Sarah wiped the rain from her face and stared at the possum, who was ambling slowly off toward the pond as if it didn't have a care in the world. But it knew where dinner was now. If she let it go, it would come back, maybe kill one of her chickens before she could kill it.

With a sick feeling in her stomach, she said, "Dead."

A second later, blue-and-orange fire burst from the gun barrel. The explosion was deafening. Sarah jerked even though she'd been expecting the blast.

The possum dropped dead in its tracks, and Morgan turned to face her, a grin on his lips. "You always shoot something that small with a thirty-thirty? It's a little like swatting flies with a two-by-four."

Sarah grinned back at him through the light drizzle and shrugged. "It was handy."

When she went back inside the chicken house to make sure there were no other surprises, Morgan didn't follow. A moment later she heard hammering and went out to find him nailing the broken door shut.

"That'll hold it for tonight," he said. "I'll put a new hinge on in the morning."

"Thanks, but you don't need to do that. You've done enough work around here. I'll fix it."

Morgan stared at her a moment. Lightning flashed overhead. "If it's all the same to you, I'd rather do this than sit around doing nothing."

Sarah opened her mouth to say it wasn't necessary for him to help out around the place. In fact, the work he'd been doing made her uncomfortable. It would be so easy for her to come to rely on him and his help. It would only make it that much harder when he took the kids and left in a few days.

She never got the chance to speak, however. Just then the sky opened up and dumped on them.

"Let's go," Morgan shouted through the deluge.

On the way past the chicken house door, he reached in and flicked off the light and swung the door closed with one hand, while tugging her in his wake with the other, all without losing stride. They dashed through the gate, got jumped on by two wet, excited dogs, and sprinted to the back porch. Sarah swore her feet never touched the ground the whole time. She and Morgan were both soaked clear through to the skin.

Morgan swung the screen door open and took both steps in one leap. With his hand still wrapped around her wrist, he lifted her over the steps and hauled her in. She landed flat against his wide, rain-slicked chest, her arms flying, her long wet hair flinging itself around the strong column of his neck.

She breathed in sharply. Nothing separated them but her thin, rain-soaked T-shirt and his wet jeans. Morgan leaned and stood the rifle in the corner, then his arms surrounded her an instant later. A flash of lightning and the glow from the kitchen window highlighted the hard planes of his dark face and gave her a glimpse of his eyes, hot and black as they devoured her. With a deep groan, he closed his eyes and squeezed her to his chest. As he lowered his head toward hers, her lips parted with a gasp. He took full advantage of it.

The frantic beating of her heart drowned out the sound of thunder and wind and rain. It also drowned out the tiny voice of common sense that screamed in the back of her mind. Sarah clung to his broad shoulders and felt her bones melt when his lips met hers. Hot, firm, silky lips. Lips to make a woman swoon. His tongue invaded her mouth, and she thought she'd die from the hot tingling that spread through her limbs.

It had been so long, *so long*. She couldn't even remember the last time a man had held her, kissed her. And she wasn't sure she'd *ever* been kissed like this before.

Morgan's hands were everywhere on her body, and she reveled in the knowledge that his heart pounded just as hard as hers. When he pressed himself against her she felt the long, hard length of his desire.

This was madness! It had to stop, and stop now, before it went any further.

But she didn't want it to stop. She wanted to stay there in his arms and hold him. She wanted to cling to his lips forever, to savor the taste of him, the strength of him, the trembling of his knees. Or was it her own knees that trembled? When he tore his mouth away, she gave a sharp cry of denial.

Morgan took his hands from her hips, grasped her shoulders, and pushed her away. She wasn't ready to stop. She wanted more. Those deep, dark eyes of his caught the glow from the kitchen light and seemed to swallow her. Then, while she watched, all expression, all hint of passion drained from his face. She was left staring at a blank mask.

He dropped his hands from her shoulders and took a step back. A heated flush stung her cheeks. Lord, what had she done? He was practically a stranger. He was the enemy. The man who'd come to steal her children. How could she have responded like that to him?

A gust of wind sent a barrage of cold raindrops pelting through the porch screen. She wrapped her arms around her stomach and shivered.

Morgan stared at her a long moment, then muttered, "Damn." He turned away and entered the house, his wet shoes squishing with every step.

Sarah died a little with each squish.

FOUR

After a nearly sleepless night, Sarah got up and dressed slowly. How was she supposed to act around Morgan after last night? Had that kiss really been that . . . devastating, or was her memory playing tricks on her? Maybe there was more truth than she cared to admit in the old saying about lonely, love-starved widows.

Ridiculous. She may have lacked adult male companionship for the past two years, but so what? That was no reason to make a big deal out of a single kiss. Right? *Right*.

She'd just act like nothing had happened, that's what she'd do. The look on Morgan's face before he'd left her standing on the porch last night indicated he'd wished it hadn't happened, so she'd just play along with him. That was the smart thing to do. It was the only thing she *could* do.

Sarah squared her shoulders and left her room. When Morgan joined the children and her for breakfast, she knew she'd been right. He greeted the kids, nodded at her, and acted just as casual as you please.

But it wasn't as easy as she'd thought, this pretending. The instant she saw him she felt her face heat up. Great. She was blushing.

During the rest of the day she didn't have to worry about blushing around Morgan. All she had to do was remind herself who he was and why he was there. She was able to act perfectly normal around him. The kiss was entirely forgotten. If her attitude toward him was on the cool side, if her words were short and brisk, well . . . what could he expect? He'd come to her home to rip her world apart. She didn't owe him kindness; she didn't owe him friendship; and she didn't owe him kisses.

If she could keep busy, she could put him out of her head. If only her damned lips would quit tingling. With a muffled oath, she headed for the garden.

The tassels on most of the corn were dry and shriveled. Picking, shucking, freezing, and canning took all her energy. She gave it gladly. If she concentrated hard enough, it took her mind off Morgan Foster. By the time the rest of the corn was ripe in a couple of weeks, he'd be gone.

No matter how Sarah wished it wouldn't, July Fourth came. The children had never whipped through their chores so fast. Sarah did her best to forget that this would be her last day with them. She didn't want to ruin these final precious hours. But still, she was surprised to find herself caught up in their excitement.

She actually grinned as they all piled into her station wagon. No one wanted to sprawl out behind the backseat for this trip; they all wanted to sit in the front. When all the scrambling was over, Wes and Jeff were in the front seat with her. Morgan, Angie, and the twins more than filled the back seat. Jeff and Angie each carefully held a shoe box containing a turtle.

Before backing out of the drive, Sarah gave one last glance into the backseat to make sure everyone was settled. Morgan grinned at her. Actually grinned! She grinned back.

It was going to be a good day. It might be her last good one for a long time, but it was going to be wonderful. She could feel it.

Twenty minutes later she pulled up in the shade of a huge pecan tree at Chandler's Tilghman Park, where State Highway Eighteen met old U.S. 66, and everyone piled out. Everyone except Angie. Angie took her time scooting across the seat, carefully balancing the box containing Speedy the Turtle, biting her lower lip in concentration. Sarah watched Morgan clench his fists to keep from reaching out to help his youngest daughter.

Finally Angie made her way out of the car, and as they crossed the street to the park, they heard the call for all entrants in the turtle races to sign up beneath the big oak next to the Kiwanis building.

"That's us, that's us, Jeffy!" Angie cried. "Come on, hurry, hurry. We'll be late. Come on, you guys."

In response, the whole family hurried toward the appropriate tree. Chandler people took their turtle racing seriously. Sarah grinned as she watched Morgan take in the surroundings and the setup.

In the dirt beneath the tree were two white chalk circles, one within the other. The outer circle was about eight feet across. The "track announcer" was calling over his portable loudspeaker for the different age groups to sign up.

Parents shouted instructions to nonattentive children. The children—those who planned to participate—were busy whispering encouragements in little turtle ears.

"Track conditions today are dry and fast," the announcer claimed. Morgan burst out laughing. Sarah didn't know which she enjoyed more—the children's excitement, or Morgan's. Both were contagious.

The youngest age group, which included Angie, was called first. "Jockeys, bring your mounts to the starting circle."

Angie, along with the other participants, placed her turtle in the inner circle. When the announcer fired the starting gun, pandemonium broke loose.

Sarah was torn between watching Angie scream at Speedy to "Go! Go! Go, Speedy!" or watching Morgan watch Angie.

The turtles themselves didn't seem to think much of all the commotion. Some went in circles, some went back and forth across the inner circle, never heading toward the outer "finish line," while two of them refused to even come out of their shells.

One of the latter, unfortunately, was Speedy.

Angie was frantic. "Come on, Speedy! Get outa there and run! Wessy, he won't run!" The poor child was nearly in tears. Then suddenly Angie swiped at her eyes, put her hands on her little hips, and shouted, "Okay, dummy, don't run. But it's turtle soup for you!'

As if he understood the threat, Speedy chose that instant to poke his head out of his shell. He blinked his little beady turtle eyes slowly and looked from side to side. Angie was down on her hands and knees just inches outside the finish line. She was begging now. "Please, Speedy?"

Speedy stretched one clawed foot out, then another, slowly, one at a time, until all four feet rested on the ground. One of his competitors crawled slowly back within the inner circle and withdrew into its shell. The little boy next to Angie started crying.

Sarah glanced at the other turtles. They were all still inside the large outer circle, but one was perilously close to crossing the line and winning the race. Poor Angie. She'd looked forward to this all year. How was she going to take the disappointment the loss was sure to bring?

But just then, as though struck by lightning, Speedy took off. "Go, Speedy!" That was from Wes, standing over Angie. Morgan squatted beside Angie, and Sarah could see him struggle to keep from shouting.

But Speedy the Turtle didn't need any more encouragement. He headed at top turtle speed straight for the finish line. The lead turtle was in his way, but Speedy didn't care. He crawled up over the other turtle's back, slid down its face, and stepped across the finish line, then stopped.

Angie swooped him up with a shout and kissed him right on the face. "You did it! You did it!"

The little girl was so excited, she turned and flung herself into Morgan's arms, Speedy dangling down Morgan's back in her haphazard grasp.

Sarah cheered with the rest of the crowd, even as a lump rose in her throat at the look on Morgan's face. He had his eyes scrunched shut and was grimacing as though in pain. Yet Sarah knew what he was feeling. This was the first time Angie had ever touched him.

Sarah blinked to clear her vision, then slapped her hands over her mouth to keep the sudden laughter from bursting out. On the back of Morgan's shirt, directly beneath Speedy's green little shell, a wet spot formed and grew wider and wider!

Morgan's shoulders stiffened. Sarah glanced around. Wes and the other kids were doubled over laughing, pointing at their father's back. She couldn't help it then. She dropped her hands and burst out laughing.

The judge called for the winners to come forward and accept their prizes—first, second, and third place ribbons. Angie pulled out of Morgan's arms and plopped the turtle into his hand. Sarah would have given everything she owned to have had a camera at that moment to capture the look on Morgan's face when he realized what the turtle had just done to him, was still doing now in his hand.

"I thought they were supposed to do that *before* the race," he said with a grimace.

Angie dashed back, waving her blue ribbon in the air, just as the next race was called. When that one ended, it was Jeff's turn. His turtle, whom he called Mr. T, didn't do as well as Speedy, but Jeff was happy with his third place ribbon.

Afterward they wandered through the park and checked out all the activities. There was horseshoe pitching, an axe-throwing exhibition, a dunk-the-teacher ball-throwing game, square dancing, Frisbee throwing, and, inside the American Legion building, behind a sign that read, "Quiet, Men At Think," a chess tournament.

And there was food. Hot dogs and watermelon, barbecued ribs and watermelon, chili and watermelon, corn-on-the-cob. And watermelon.

An hour before dark, the exhausted group headed for home. Once there, Sarah gathered up quilts and insect repellent while Wes filled an ice chest with soft drinks and a pitcher of Kool Aid.

"What's all this for?" Morgan wanted to know.

Sarah smiled. The tension between them was gone. She was glad to feel at ease around him and refused to think about tomorrow. "We're going to watch the fireworks."

"Whose fireworks?"

"Everybody's." At his puzzled look, she explained. "It's tradition around here. At dark on the Fourth of July, we meet the Hudspeths at the top of the hill between our two houses. From there we can see the fireworks from Chandler, Meeker, Prague, and even Shawnee. We've got the best fireworks-watching hill around."

"Wait till you see, Dad," Wes told him. "It's the best part of the whole day."

"The best?" Morgan grinned at his oldest son.

"Well, it sure beats having a turtle pee down your back."

Morgan threw back his head and laughed. Sarah stared in awe, as she'd done all day. When he laughed, the hard lines on his face disappeared and his eyes sparkled. He looked softer, nicer . . . younger. And Lord help her, even more devastatingly, breathtakingly handsome.

They loaded the quilts and ice chest into the small trailer Rob had hitched to the riding mower. Angie clambered up over the side to ride in style, while the others walked up to the top of the hill.

The Hudspeths, with their ice-cream freezer, were already there. Sarah introduced Morgan to Rita and Barry.

"So," Barry said after shaking hands, "you're the father of Sarah's children."

Morgan nearly swallowed his tongue, then managed a smile. "I . . . uh . . . guess you've been to the bank, right?"

Barry laughed and shook his head. He started to answer, but Rita interrupted him.

"Feed store."

Morgan winced. "How—"

"What feed store?" Sarah wanted to know. "What's going on here?"

Barry and Rita laughed again, and Morgan was forced to tell about the woman at the bank.

Sarah rolled her eyes and groaned. "It had to be Myrna Selznick. Lord help us, it's all over town by now."

"Take it easy, girl," Rita said. "At this point it's just friendly speculation. It hasn't turned vicious. Yet," she added with a wiggle of her brows.

"So what are your plans? Will you be leaving soon?" Barry asked Morgan.

Morgan watched, dismayed, as Sarah's face paled. He wanted to answer that it was none of Hudspeth's business. But the look on the man's face was one of simple, friendly curiosity, open and guileless. Morgan just shrugged.

"You oughta stick around. This is just about the best damned place in the world to raise kids. Clean air, good schools, low crime. Those things are hard to find these days."

Sarah turned away, shoulders stiff, to help Rita dish out the ice cream. Morgan forced another smile. "Thanks for the advice. I'll keep it in mind."

Everyone sprawled on the quilts and ate the Hudspeths' homemade vanilla ice cream while waiting for full darkness and fireworks. The air was filled with the excited chatter of children retelling the day, the loud droning buzz of cicadas, and the sometimes choking smell of insect repellent.

Morgan felt deep, strong emotions squeeze his heart when Angie wiggled around until she sat between Sarah and him. She'd touched him today. His Angie had finally touched him. Not only touched, but hugged. It confused him, even scared him a little, to think something so small as a child's touch could be so powerful.

Sarah, too, had touched something in him today, in an equally strong, yet different way. Her answering smiles, her carefree laughter, had set something loose within him, breached some barrier he hadn't even known was there. And her strength and courage were evident in every smile, in every touch she gave his children. She knew, because they'd talked about it, that he and his children would leave tomorrow. Yet not once had she allowed that knowledge to show on her face.

But would he take the children and leave tomorrow? Could he? They'd seemed so much like a real, complete family today. What would they become without Sarah?

Yet he knew they couldn't stay. There was no point in delaying the inevitable.

"There goes one!" Wes shouted.

In the east, where he pointed, a single streak of light shot upward into the night sky, then burst into a shower of red and white. The children cheered.

"There's another one," Connie called, pointing to the north. Another streak rose, then exploded, sending brilliant sparkles drifting toward earth.

"I can't see, I can't see," Angie complained.

"Come here then," Morgan said. He stood and swung her up to sit on his shoulders.

She shrieked with delight. "I'm bigger than anybody!"

By the time the fireworks were over, Angie was asleep in his arms. Even the mower didn't wake her when Rob started it to head back.

At the house, Morgan turned to Sarah, Angie still asleep in his arms. "It's been a long time since I put a kid to bed. I could use some help."

Sarah nodded without looking at him, and followed. She was withdrawing from him. The day of fun and laughter was over, and tomorrow he'd take his children and leave. Withdrawal was her defense. He understood. He understood, but he didn't like it.

It was a hell of a situation, he thought as he climbed the stairs to the children's bedrooms. She'd taken in his children when no one else would, and treated them, loved them, as if they were her own. In repayment, he was going to hurt her. She didn't deserve that.

But what else could he do? They were his children. He loved them, too, and they belonged with him. He couldn't afford to feel sorry for her. She would hate that. She wanted his children, not his pity.

Sarah pulled the covers aside, and Morgan laid Angie on the bed. They both reached at once to remove the same tennis shoe. Their hands touched. They both jerked away. Morgan looked into Sarah's big gray eyes, startled.

It had happened again. That searing jolt of heat and electricity and awareness he'd felt when they shook hands that first day. That tingling down his spine and rapid thudding of his heart as when he'd held her rain-soaked body close to his and kissed her in the dark on the back porch.

Before he could do anything more than stare at her, she gasped, straightened, and dashed from the room. Morgan closed his eyes and took a deep breath. When he reached again to remove Angie's shoe, his hands were trembling.

A moment later, Sarah came back with a wet washcloth and gently wiped the ice cream and Kool-Aid from Angie's face. Without looking at him or speaking, she proceeded to help him undress his youngest. Then she practically ran from the room.

After making certain all the kids were in bed, Morgan went downstairs and found Sarah frantically rinsing dishes at the sink.

He'd felt a dozen different emotions when their hands had accidentally met. Pity wasn't anywhere on the list. He wanted to talk to her, to understand, to explore what he was feeling. At the same time, he wanted to run. He didn't belong here on this farm, with this woman.

But still he reached out and placed a hand on her shoulder. "Sarah?"

She stiffened, then tried to shrug his hand away. "Don't."

He reached around her and took the plate from her white-knuckled grip, set it in the sink, and shut off the water. Then he turned her around to face him. "Look at me, Sarah," he said softly.

She shuddered once, then slowly raised her gaze to his. The gray pain and despair in her eyes nearly took his breath away. He'd come here all full of righteous indignation, determined to destroy the creature who had abused his children. But no one had abused them. Instead, Sarah had loved them. Still, he was destroying her.

He lowered his forehead to rest against hers. "I'm sorry, Sarah," he whispered. "So damned sorry." He heard her whimper, and he kissed the hair at her temple. "I'm sorry you lost your parents and your husband." He wrapped his arms around her and pulled her to his chest. "I'm sorry you never had children of your own." He kissed her forehead, then one eyebrow. "I'm sorry you came to love my children so much." He kissed the other brow, then a cheek, then her nose. "I'm sorry I have to take them away. I'm sorry for everything," he said.

Unable and unwilling to deny himself any longer, he brushed his lips across hers. "Everything," he whispered, "but this."

He kissed her then, full on the lips. Her mouth trembled beneath his, then opened its sweetness to his questing tongue. She was so incredibly warm and giving. She held nothing back from him, and he took all she offered.

She'd taken his children into her home, into her heart, and changed their lives with her love. She could do that for him. She could take him into her heart, take his body into hers, and give him a peace and emotional security the likes of which he'd never known. He knew she could. It was all there in her fingers that threaded through his hair, in the way her body perfectly molded to his, in the way she melted in his arms and whimpered in her throat.

The sounds she made, the way she moved against him, threatened his control. He'd only meant to comfort her. But now he wanted more. So much, much more. And she was giving it to him, responding to his very breath. Frantically his hands roamed over her, trying to pull her even closer, desperate to hang on to whatever sense this made. Behind his closed lids, fireworks exploded.

She was all storm and fire in his arms. Yet at the same time she was the only calm, sane thing in a world that constantly tried to tear itself apart. The eye of his own personal hurricane.

He felt his desire ready to explode, his sudden, fierce need of this woman threaten to overwhelm him. Slowly, slowly, with more willpower than he knew he had or even wanted to have, he drew away from her.

She looked up at him, passion glazing her gray eyes, and it was all he could do to keep from kissing her again. Kissing her, and more.

Then suddenly her eyes cleared and widened—with something he could only describe as horror. She covered her mouth with both hands and ran from the kitchen, leaving him standing there with empty, aching arms.

He wanted . . . Hell, he wanted too much.

But was it too much? Or only too soon?

He went to bed and lay awake for hours.

Foster, you've got to get your ass outa here and away from her, and fast, buddy.

She wasn't his type. Not at all. He'd never fallen for a wholesome, down-to-earth farm girl. Even if she was beautiful. Hell, he didn't even *like* wholesome, down-to-earth farm girls.

They were—no, *she* was—too open, too vulnerable, too easily hurt. He was too cynical, too careless, too callous.

So why does the earth move beneath your feet when you kiss her, huh, buddy?

Why, indeed.

He didn't really *have* to leave tomorrow. Should he stay, just to see what developed between them? She was a beautiful, passionate woman with a loving heart. Relationships were built every day on less than passion.

Just look at his marriage to Joyce. They hadn't even had that much going for them in the beginning, and they still managed to be . . . satisfied, sometimes even happy, for a good twelve years. Well, a good ten years. The last two had been a little rough. But still, ten years was a long time.

The only guarantee in life that even came close was the one for six years or sixty thousand miles—whichever came first.

He ground his teeth. He knew he didn't want to settle for another stretch of "satisfied, sometimes even happy." Not with Sarah. It would never work. He had to get off this farm, away from her. Soon. Now.

You know why you're afraid, don't you, buddy?

Afraid?

Scared spitless would be more like it.

Scared spitless. Yes. That's what he was. He was scared that Sarah only saw the attraction between them as a way to hang on to his children. She might even come to care for Morgan Foster, father of five. But what about Morgan Foster, the man?

He'd never be satisfied to stay in the background and take whatever affection she had left over after lavishing it on the kids. Never again would he put himself in the position of being on the outside looking in. It was too lonely, too painful. She'd have to want him for himself, or not at all.

So how are you ever going to know, if you up and leave, huh?

Ah, shut up.

* * *

Sarah had been drunk once when she was sixteen. She and Rita had sneaked into Rita's grandfather's homemade beer. They'd drank so much that both of them had been as sick as dogs before the night was over. And then, the next morning, Sarah had experienced the one and only hangover she'd ever had in her life.

Now Sarah felt cheated. Here she was, feeling every bit as miserable as she had with that hangover, but this time it was merely from crying herself to sleep instead of drinking. She'd been cheated out of those few hours of euphoria a person's supposed to have before the pain sets in.

She groaned and climbed out of bed. Maybe she hadn't been cheated after all. This time around she hadn't been forced to hug the commode half the night.

And there had been euphoria. Yesterday had turned out just as wonderful as she'd predicted. And then there was last night. Last night in Morgan's arms, for a few brief, magical moments.

She groaned again when she looked in the mirror. She might as well have been on a drunk. She sure looked the part.

Her face was pale, her hair was matted, and her eyes . . . Oh! The flesh around them was puffy and swollen, but the real kicker was the part of her eyes surrounding her irises. The part that was supposed to be white.

What they were was red. Well, actually an overall pinkish color with tiny red streaks zigzagging everywhere. Good Lord, her eyeballs looked like a road map of Georgia.

They felt like sandpaper.

She crawled into the shower and let the cool spray pound against her face and head. Afterward she decided she felt a little better. Until she remembered what day it was.

Now, she thought with a lurch in her heart, she had to go out there and cook one more big breakfast for the children. For the last time. And then she had to help them pack. And then she had to tell them good-bye. With a smile.

A tear formed in her eye.

She couldn't do it. She might possibly live through everything else. Maybe. But she couldn't smile.

Sarah swallowed back her tears. She'd shed enough last night to flood the creek. She pulled on faded jeans and T-shirt, socks and boots, and forced herself out of her room and into the kitchen.

There was a sick feeling growing in her stomach. She'd never be able to eat.

Wes bounded in the back door. "I've already let the chickens out."

She couldn't smile. She swallowed. "Thanks." *Oh God oh God, Wes, you're going to leave today and I may never see you again.*

To keep from bawling like a calf stuck in the mud, Sarah poked her head into the refrigerator and started pulling things out for breakfast. Bacon, eggs, butter, milk . . . .

Somehow breakfast got cooked and served. When Sarah took her place at the table, she refused to look up from her plate. The children were having an ordinary breakfast conversation, as though they had no plans to leave today. Maybe Morgan hadn't told them this was the day.

Because she dawdled with her food, Morgan finished eating before she did. He got up from the table and placed a call from the wall phone behind her chair.

Long distance. She could tell by the number of buttons he pushed. Great. He was taking his kids and leaving her a phone bill.

Calm down, Sarah. You'll live. Somehow.

She tried not to listen to him, but couldn't help it. He was asking about someone named Coop.

"What do you mean you haven't heard! How long's he been down there? Well, call me the minute you hear anything . . . Yeah, I'll get you your report." He then gave Sarah's phone number. "I don't know. Hang on."

Morgan nudged her shoulder. Sarah whirled around to look at him. He had his hand over the mouthpiece. "He wants to know how long I'll be at this number."

She stared at him. The conversations around the table halted abruptly, except for the one Angie was having with her food. What was he talking about? Was he talking hours, or days? Did this mean he wasn't leaving yet? Trying to act nonchalant, she shrugged. "Suit yourself."

Morgan held her gaze for a long moment, and she returned it, puzzled, trying to understand what was happening.

He raised the mouthpiece to his lips again. "I'll be here . . . indefinitely."

"All right!" Wes shouted. The others grinned. Sarah just stared at Morgan. And he stared back.

When he hung up, he stopped beside Sarah. "I've got a report to write. You don't happen to have a typewriter around, do you?"

It was slowly sinking in. He was staying. The children were staying. But why? What had changed his mind?

"Sarah?" he said. "A typewriter?"

She shook herself. If he could act so cool about it, then so could she. "A typewriter and a computer. Connie, show your dad the office."

He stayed in the office all day. He came out long enough for supper, then went back. Sarah never had a chance to talk to him. On her way to check on the kids after they were in bed that night, she passed the closed office door next to his bedroom and heard the clacking of the computer keyboard.

When she came back down a few minutes later, she turned on a late movie and decided to outwait him. They simply had to talk. She had to know why he was staying.

Perhaps it was convenient for him to stay here. That would save him from having to relocate the children. But he couldn't stay here indefinitely, they both knew that. So why not go and get the move over with? Did he think staying longer would be easier on the children? Or, knowing how she felt about the children, was he staying because he felt sorry for her.

Maybe he thought if he stayed long enough, she might change her mind and sell the farm to him. That way he wouldn't have to leave at all.

* * *

Morgan rolled his stiff shoulders and rubbed his eyes. Enough. He saved what he'd been working on and turned off the computer.

He'd decided to stay and go slowly with Sarah, to explore whatever it was that happened between them when they touched. But he wanted to go slowly, not rush her. The report was a good excuse to keep away from her. A dozen times today he'd nearly quit typing and gone in search of her.

But he kept reminding himself . . . Slowly. He had to go slowly.

Slowly's one thing, buddy. Staying completely away from her isn't slow, it's backward.

When he left the office a few minutes later, he found her asleep on the couch.

Damn.

It wasn't fair for her to look so soft and warm and vulnerable. And inviting. He stood beside her and smiled slightly at her skewed ponytail and rumpled clothes.

"Sarah, my girl, you're a mess," he whispered. "A lovable, adorable mess."

The urge to hold her, to cuddle her in his arms and have her snuggle up against him overpowered his otherwise good sense. He picked her up and carried her to her room. On the way, she sighed. And snuggled.

When he placed her on her raised bed, it gave. He froze. *Oh, Lord.* Sarah in his arms was trouble enough. But Sarah in his arms on a waterbed—a warm, *undulating* waterbed.

In the darkness, lit only by the filtered glow of the outside yard light, he rested his forehead against hers, trying to summon up the willpower to pull his arms from beneath her pliant body and walk away. He *had* to walk away.

From somewhere, he found the strength. He stood next to the bed, looking down at her. She sighed and crossed her arms as if she were cold.

Damn. He couldn't leave her like that. With his teeth clenched so hard his jaws hurt, he slipped off the fuzzy house shoes she always wore indoors. Then came her socks. Small socks, for small, delicate feet.

With more control than he knew he had, he unsnapped her jeans, lowered the zipper, and, as gently as he could, trying desperately not to awaken her—how the hell would he ever explain himself? —he tugged off her pants. She could damn well sleep in the rest of her clothes.

Her long, slender legs gleamed pale in the dim light. Were they as soft and silky as they looked? He stopped himself just short of touching to find out.

She was lying on top of the covers, and he was afraid to pick her up to pull them from beneath her. Afraid he might wake her, and afraid he might not be able to let her go a second time. He spied a quilt draped across the foot of the bed and gratefully pulled it up to her chin. His hands were shaking.

As if the hounds of hell were after him, he fled.

It didn't take Sarah long the next morning to figure out what had happened. She must have fallen asleep on the couch, and someone had carried her to bed. She had a vague, disturbing memory of—*Oh, good Lord*—of someone pulling off her jeans!

It also didn't take her long to figure out just who that someone was.

New experiences were supposed to be exciting. This one was downright embarrassing. Why hadn't he just left her where he'd found her? And how, in the name of heaven, was she supposed to face a man, a near stranger, after he'd partially undressed her?

It wasn't any easier than she'd feared when she finally came face-to-face with him at breakfast. He gave no indication at all of having performed such an intimate service as putting her to bed.

At least not the few times she chanced a look at him. Which wasn't often. Yet every time she did, she felt heat stinging her cheeks.

When breakfast was over, Sarah watched Morgan closet himself in the office again. He hadn't said anything to her other than "Good morning."

As soon as the dishes were done and the kitchen was clean, she shooed the kids out to play. It was time she and Morgan Foster had a talk. This just wasn't going to work. He couldn't stay here any longer.

FIVE

Sarah tapped on the office door, then, without waiting for a response, she opened it and walked in.

Morgan sat at the computer with his back to the door. Slowly he looked at her over his shoulder, his fingers falling motionless on the keyboard.

She'd finally cornered him. It was now or never. "I need to talk to you."

"About what?"

As if he didn't know. She closed the door and leaned back against it, her hands behind her on the doorknob. "Did you . . . put me to bed last night?"

He swiveled the desk chair around until he faced her. "No need to thank me," he said with a slight smile. "It was my pleasure."

His words triggered a replay in her mind of soft denim sliding down her legs. She felt her cheeks heat up. This was definitely a dumb idea. It was time to change the subject. "You can't stay here, Morgan."

He quirked a brow at her. "You throwing me out?"

Out? Did she really want him to leave? Did she really want him to take his smile, his warmth, his children, and leave? "No, it's just that . . ."

"Yes?"

He had to go. She had to stop thinking about herself and what she wanted. "Well, staying here isn't going to do the children any good. I don't mean to tell you what's best for them—"

"Why stop now?"

Sarah took a deep breath. She would not lose her temper. She simply would not. "I mean, they are your children, and—"

"You finally realized that, did you?"

She gritted her teeth. "Do you want to have this conversation or don't you?"

"Not particularly. I'm busy."

"Well, excuse me," she snapped, forgetting her promise of seconds ago. "I thought your children's welfare was important to you. I guess I was wrong."

Morgan heaved a sigh. "All right, I'll bite. What does my children's welfare have to do with this?"

"If you'd cut the sarcastic remarks, you might find out."

He didn't want to find out. He didn't want to have this conversation at all. Besides, she was so much fun to rile, maybe because she didn't seem to rile all that easily. But if he pointed out how much fun he was having, she'd probably belt him one. He sat back in the chair and folded his arms, waiting for her to continue.

"You need to get the kids settled in their new

home. They need to be able to get established in a new neighborhood. School will be starting again before you know it, and Wes, I'm sure, will want to try out for the football team at his new school. Tryouts are held weeks before classes start. The longer you keep them here, the less time they'll have to—"

"I'm sure glad you don't want to tell me what's best for my children."

Sarah leaned her head back against the door and closed her eyes in frustration. "Don't do this, Morgan. Not to me, not to them. You might, and I say *might*, have yourself a good time for a while. But the rest of us will only be hurt by your games. I know my feelings don't matter to you, but theirs should."

She left before he could comment, closing the door softly behind her. He stared at it for a long time, wondering if she was right. Was he playing games? If not, then just what in the hell was he doing? He stared at the door as if expecting it to give him an answer, but there was no answer.

All he knew was that Sarah drew him, pulled at something deep inside him, and he couldn't leave. Not yet. Not until he understood.

He got up and followed her. He found her in the laundry room putting a load of clothes in the washer.

"I'm not playing any games, Sarah."

Startled, Sarah jerked her arm out of the washer and whacked her elbow on the rim. "Damn!' She grabbed her elbow, her face a grimace of pain.

"I'm sorry," he offered. "I didn't mean to startle you."

She just glared at him and kept rubbing her elbow.

"Here." He brushed her hand away and rubbed at the sore spot himself. Gradually her face relaxed. He used his other hand to massage her stiff shoulder.

She stared up at him, her eyes wide, gray, and wary. Eyes he could look into forever. Without thinking, he lowered his head toward hers. Her tongue came out and swiped nervously at her bottom lip. He nearly groaned.

"If this isn't a game," she said breathlessly, "then what is it?"

When her words sank in and he realized what he was doing, what he was about to do, he jerked his hands away as if he'd been burned. With a curse, he spun and paced to the door and back. "I'm sorry."

She turned around and finished pushing clothes into the washer. She added detergent, set the dial, and started the machine. He had to step aside or get trampled when she stalked through the door.

He followed. "Look, Sarah, I just want . . ."

She paused and looked at him over her shoulder. "You want?"

Damnit, this wasn't working. She was about as trusting as a wild animal. But then, if she knew what he really wanted, she'd have every reason not to trust him. He needed a legitimate excuse to stay near her, one she would buy. He should be ashamed of himself for the one he'd just come up with, but he wasn't.

"I want to get to know my kids again. It's been

over four years since I've seen them. If I just take them away from here, away from you, they'll be so upset they won't give me a chance. Just let us stay for a while. Let me spend some time with them here, where they feel at home."

"That's going to be a bit hard to do, isn't it, with you shut up in the office all day every day."

She had him there. "You're right. I can work on my report after they're in bed at night."

Sarah felt her resolve melting. He was right. It would be better for all of them if they stayed here awhile. Better for them, worse for her. How much longer could she take his nearness? How long could she fight the strong attraction that pulled her toward him without making a complete fool of herself?

She knew if she gave in and let him know how she felt, it would be the biggest mistake of her life. Because no matter what happened between them, she knew that one day soon, he'd be gone. He'd take his children and his warmth and his smile and leave. And she'd be left alone. Totally, completely alone.

"How . . . how long do you think all this will take?"

Morgan felt the tightness in his chest ease. She wasn't throwing him out. "I don't know," he said, forcing a shrug. "I'd like to just play it by ear."

Instead of answering, Sarah turned away from him and went to her room. He didn't follow.

That evening when he joined the others in the living room to watch television, Sarah left the room. He found her later, back in the laundry room, this time folding clothes instead of washing them.

The next night it happened again. He walked in, she walked out. She had mending to do.

The third night, she cleaned the oven. By the fourth night, Morgan had had enough. When she left the kids in the living room and made for the back porch, he followed. He knew she heard him open the door and step out, but she didn't turn to face him. She stood staring out into the dark yard with her arms folded and shoulders hunched, as if she were cold in the hot night air.

"Why do I get the feeling you're avoiding me?" he asked softly.

"I don't know." She spoke to the screen wire, not to him.

"Maybe because every time I walk into a room, you leave out the nearest door?"

"You're imagining things."

"Am I?"

She sighed. "I'm not avoiding you. I'm just trying to give you some time alone with the kids. That's why you're here, isn't it? To spend time with them, get to know them?"

Morgan stuffed his hands into his pockets to keep from grabbing her by the shoulders and shaking her. For a long moment the only sounds were those of crickets chirping, cicadas buzzing, and June bugs hitting the kitchen window screen. "I could use a little help with that."

She glanced at him, then looked away. "What kind of help?"

"With Angie." The situation with his youngest daughter had improved dramatically since the Fourth of July, but not nearly enough to suit him.

"She's coming around," Sarah said. "She just needs a little more time."

"And how much time do I have, before you ask me to leave?" She still had her back to him. Why the hell didn't she turn around?

"As I recall, I *did* ask you to leave. You ignored me. So you're still here, to get reacquainted with your children. Suppose you tell me how long that's going to take."

"Damnit, Sarah, look at me." But she didn't. In frustration, he grabbed her by the shoulder and forced her to turn around. "You know the kids aren't the only reason I stayed."

She lowered her arms slowly to her sides. "They aren't?" He wished he could read the expression on her face, but there were too many shadows on the porch.

"No, they aren't."

"Then . . . then why?"

His heartbeat was like thunder in his ears. She was so close he could feel her breath on his chin. He stepped closer. Without thinking, he cupped his hands around her neck. "Why?"

"Why."

He saw her swallow, felt it beneath the heels of his hands. Her lips were much too soft, too close, too tempting. He brushed them with his. "Because of this," he answered, turning the brief touch into a full, passionate kiss.

Before she could do anything about it, Sarah

was responding to him. The coldness she'd been feeling for days was seared away by her own passion for him.

Because of this, he'd said. He was staying because of this. Because of what happened every time they touched. He felt it, too, and that knowledge sent her heart soaring.

All too soon, as far as she was concerned, he pulled his lips from hers. It was then she realized they were both gasping for breath.

Morgan groaned and buried his face in that delicious spot where her slim neck met her soft shoulder. "I can't leave yet, Sarah. Please don't ask me to leave."

Oh God, Sarah thought. How was she supposed to resist a plea like that? And why, dear Lord, should she even try? "You . . . don't want to leave?"

Morgan felt her warm, slender fingers touch his nape. He shuddered. His "no" came out more as a groan than a word. *No, I don't want to leave. No, it's not right, not smart. No, don't put your lips on my cheek. No, Sarah, no.*

He raised his head until their mouths met again, wet and wild and clinging. If he didn't stop soon—He tore his lips away and leaned his forehead on hers. Their harsh breathing covered up the normal night sounds.

When they both calmed, he raised his head to look at her. He turned her until he could see her face in the light from the kitchen window. Then he nearly lost control.

Her eyes were glazed with hungry passion, her

lips soft, wet, and swollen from the pressure of his. But he still couldn't tell what she was thinking.

The game, if there was one, was over. He had to know where he stood with her. He took a deep breath for courage. "So, do I go? Or do I stay?"

She looked at him a long moment without answering. He almost gave up hope of a response when her fingers unwound themselves from his hair and pressed lightly against his lips. He kissed them.

"I think," she whispered, "because of this . . ." She traced the outline of his mouth. ". . . you should stay."

He let his breath out.

When she smiled at him, his heart soared.

Because of this . . .

Sarah relived that kiss a dozen times during the night and woke with a grin. He was staying! Morgan Foster was staying *because of this*.

When she got out of bed there was a definite bounce to her step. She wouldn't dwell on the particulars. It was enough for now to know that whatever it was that had happened between them when they kissed, he felt it, too. And it was powerful enough to get him to change his mind about leaving. And powerful enough to rid her of any apprehension, any misgivings she'd had.

She loved him! The realization was shocking. Exhilarating. Even a little scary. But it was a good scary.

She stretched her arms over her head and grinned. She'd never expected to love a man again, but here it was. She was in love with Morgan Foster.

He might not love her in return, but he felt something, she knew, or he wouldn't still be here.

Thank you God, thank you God, thank you God.

She whistled as she started preparing breakfast. Connie came to help and added words to the song. Before the bacon was done, Rob and Angie joined in.

When he stepped out of the shower Morgan heard the singing and smiled. His kids were singing a Broadway show tune. Considering they lived in Oklahoma, the song was appropriate. Judging by the rhythmic clink and clank accompanying the song, the table was evidently being set to the beat of the music.

By the time he reached the kitchen, all the children were there and singing. They had already giggled, botched and improvised their way through the part where the chickens, ducks and geese needed to scurry. They'd passed the part about cows mooing in the clover. The last verse was being sung slowly, but the rush to get the food on the table was at a near-frantic pace, with everyone laughing between lyrics. It was a race. They were trying to get all the food on the table before the end of the song. The last plate was placed on the table in time with the final words.

Angie squealed and clapped her hands in delight.

"We made it!" Jeff yelled.

"Now we can eat." Rob's only concern was feeding his "monster stomach."

No one had noticed Morgan yet where he leaned

against the doorframe. He grinned and applauded the impromptu concert.

Sarah whirled to face him, a flush of pleasure on her cheeks and sparkles brighter than fireworks in her eyes. Her . . . *blue* eyes! They were. They were blue! Yet he'd known for certain that yesterday they'd been gray.

"Good morning," she said. The breathlessness in her voice nearly turned his knees to water.

Sit down, buddy, before you make a fool out of yourself.

There were times when he just couldn't argue with that damned voice in his head, and this was one of them. He sat down.

By the time he'd finished eating breakfast, Morgan had seen enough of her sparkling blue eyes and her radiant smile to set his hands to trembling. He fled to the office the first chance he got.

Sarah Collins was becoming entirely too irresistible, and Morgan Foster was becoming . . . obsessed.

Lord, have mercy.

Sarah didn't see Morgan again until supper, and by then she was nervous. It was a good kind of nervous, an exciting kind of nervous. Anticipation, that's what it was. All day long, through the laundry, the dusting, the weeding in the garden, she'd kept her eyes and ears tuned to any sight or sound of him. But he hadn't come out of the office until supper. She was sorry she'd ever told him about that damned computer.

Now here he was, sitting across the table from her with his bedroom eyes taking her breath away.

Sometime during the night she'd made up her mind to take life an hour at a time, and take—and give—whatever Morgan wanted.

It hadn't been an easy decision, or even a conscious one. She'd never had an affair before. Yet if she was reading him right, she was about to.

And there was no way she wasn't reading him right. When she swiped a dab of cheese sauce from her lower lip with her tongue, his eyes followed the movement. It was several long seconds before he raised his gaze to hers. It was all she could do to keep from dropping her fork at the heated look he gave her.

"I'll set the volleyball net up after supper if anybody wants to play," Wes said, interrupting the silent tension that had Sarah holding her breath.

"I'll play," Jeff said.

"Me, too."

"Me, too."

"Do I get to hit the ball?" Angie asked, her big brown eyes on her oldest brother.

"You get to hit the ball," he said. "How about you two?" he asked his father and Sarah. "You gonna play?"

The heat in Morgan's eyes seemed to flare as he looked at Sarah. The fork trembled in her hand.

"How about it, Sarah," Morgan asked softly. "You wanna play?"

She tried to swallow, but couldn't. "I'll play."

A slow, devilish grin spread across Morgan's face and his dark eyes glowed. "I was hoping you'd say that."

It was nothing short of a miracle that Sarah

didn't break every dish in the house while she rushed to clean up the kitchen. Especially since Morgan hung around and never took his eyes off her.

More than once she caught herself stealing glances at him and grinning. She had to control the urge to laugh out loud. Morgan Foster was pursuing her like no man had ever done before. It was the most heady feeling she'd ever experienced. She felt exhilarated and feminine and more desirable than she could ever remember feeling.

She grinned again. The next time she had him in her bedroom late at night, she'd be damned if he'd walk off and leave her while she slept!

When he held the back door open for her to go out, she purposely brushed against him. She was gratified to hear his sharp intake of breath. Two could play this game.

Wes set the volleyball net up on a flat area behind the backyard. That late in the day the two huge trees near the fence—a cottonwood and a pecan—cast long shadows that would give the players some relief from the ninety-five degree heat.

They chose up teams, with Morgan, Angie, and the twins on one side, Sarah, Wes, and Jeff on the other. Morgan would serve first.

"Are you ready over there?" he called.

"Let 'er rip," Jeff hollered.

"We're ready," Wes said.

"What about you, Sarah?" Morgan asked. "Are you ready for what I'm about to serve you?"

"Put your money where your mouth is, Foster," she called. A devil in her made her add, "I'm more than ready. I can handle anything you want to send my way."

Morgan bounced the ball once on the ground and grinned wickedly. "Is that a fact? Heads up!" And he served the ball.

Wes returned it, and the volley was on. Just as the ball sailed over the net toward him, Morgan wrapped one arm around Angie's waist and lifted her up against his hip so she could hit the ball. She more or less let it hit her, then Morgan one-handed it to keep it in the air, and Connie popped it over the net to Jeff, who slammed it directly into the net.

By the time the game ended—everyone declared it a was tie—they were all hot and sweaty and weak with laughter. A line formed at the garden hose. Morgan got more than the drink he wanted when Angie accidentally squirted him in the chest. "Oops" was all she said. Everyone else laughed, and in retaliation, Morgan turned the hose on them all.

When he passed the hose to Rob, Sarah was right behind Morgan. He turned and stumbled into her. She was never sure exactly how they ended up on the ground together with him cradled between her upraised knees, but she liked it. She liked it a lot.

"As Angie would say . . ." Morgan told her with a cocky grin, "oops."

Sarah feigned outrage. "You did that on purpose, you monster."

He raised himself on his elbows. "Who, me?"

"Yeah, you." Sarah was starting to blush and laugh. "What I'd like to know is what you hope to gain by it. Get off before you crush me." She thrust her body upward, trying to dislodge him.

His eyes widened. "Do that again," he whispered, "and I'll show you what I hope to gain."

She felt her blush deepen. "As much fun as this is, I'd like to take this opportunity to remind you that we have, at this very moment, quite an avid audience."

Morgan jerked his head up, seemingly surprised to find the kids still there.

"Get off her, Dad, before you squash her like a bug," Jeff said.

Morgan's voice was strained when he levered himself up onto hands and knees. "We'll, uh . . . pick this up . . . later."

He stood, then grasped her hand and pulled her to her feet. She wasn't a bit surprised to find her knees trembling. The man was definitely high voltage.

The man was a tease, that was all there was to it. He led her on, flirted with her, got her all stirred up, then backed away. Oh, he wanted her, Sarah had no doubt. But when it got right down to it, like late at night after the kids were in bed, when they could at least indulge in a few heated kisses, he invariably threw up barriers.

Barriers, hell. He ran. It was that simple. The man fled from her. And Sarah didn't have the slightest idea what to do about it.

She aimed the roaring vacuum cleaner out of the

formal dining room, which they used only on special occasions, into the hall that led past Morgan's room and the office, and on toward the stairs. She hoped the noise disturbed him in there with that damned computer.

As far as she knew, her ploy didn't work, for the office door never opened.

When she finished vacuuming, she changed loads in the washer and dryer—with five kids in the house, the laundry was never done—then attacked the kitchen floor with a vengeance.

If she worked hard enough, maybe she'd be so exhausted she'd actually fall asleep that night instead of tossing and turning for hours.

She hadn't had a decent night's sleep since Morgan Foster set foot on her farm. And virtually no sleep at all since they'd started playing this cat-and-mouse game.

The only thing she couldn't figure out was, which of them was the cat, and which the mouse.

The exhaustion ploy didn't work any better than the vacuum ploy. Thoughts of Morgan teased her for hours after she went to bed. The memory of his kisses refused to let her be. When, in the wee hours before dawn, she was finally able to drop off, his image followed into her dreams.

Erotic dreams.

Waking up quivering with unfulfilled desire, sweat streaking her prickly skin, was worse than not sleeping at all.

Nope. Housework wasn't the answer. The next day she decided to clean out the chicken house. Maybe all that dust and manure would clear her head.

* * *

"Why are we still here?"

Morgan inadvertently jerked on the reins at Wes's question. Spot—who the hell ever heard of a horse (a mare, no less) named Spot?—tossed her head and pranced sideways at the inattentive handling. Morgan calmed the horse while trying to come up with an answer for Wes. "You in a hurry to leave?"

"Heck no. I thought you were, though."

"Not particularly."

Wes's initial question—why were they still at Sarah's—had surprised Morgan, and it shouldn't have. He should have expected it days ago. For a man who'd spent years examining every angle of a situation and planning for every possible alternative, and a few impossible ones, he'd sure had his eyes closed this time. But then he hadn't been thinking straight since he'd first laid eyes on Sarah Collins.

"How long we gonna stay?" Wes wanted to know.

Morgan shrugged and started the Appaloosa forward at a walk. "For a while yet. I'd like to wait at least until I know Coop's okay." *And until I decide what to do about Sarah.*

"Your old army buddy? The one you used to tell me about, who saved your life in Vietnam?"

"Yeah. He should have been back by now."

"You're worried about him?"

"Some," Morgan allowed with a nod.

"Where'd he go?"

"He went looking for me."

Wes was quiet for a while. Too quiet, Morgan thought. Then Wes reined to a halt. The boy—*no, he's a young man now*—rested his hands on the saddle horn and watched a red-tailed hawk soar against the brilliant blue sky. The bird banked right on an air current and made a pass over the catfish pond.

"And if you don't hear from him?" Wes asked, his eyes still on the hawk. "What then? Will you go after him?"

It took a long time for Morgan to answer. Finally he said, "Wouldn't you?"

Wes's shoulders drooped. "That's what I thought."

Morgan's own shoulders drooped. How was he to make Wes and the others understand? He loved them and wouldn't hurt them for the world, and God knew Morgan didn't want to leave his family ever again, for any reason. But if Coop didn't come home soon, Morgan knew he'd have no choice.

"I know I promised I wouldn't leave again, and I meant it. But I had no idea Coop would be gone this long. It makes me think something's wrong. I owe him, Wes. If he needs me, I have to go."

Wes took a deep breath and squared his shoulders. "I know, Dad. Like you said, I'd do the same. Just try not to be gone so long this time, huh?"

The teasing glint, the mature understanding in Wes's eyes, sent fierce pride shooting through Morgan's veins and raised a lump in his throat. It was a moment before he could speak. "You're a pretty terrific young man, you know that?"

Wes's chest swelled at least an inch. The two grinned at each other.

"Thanks, Dad."

"Thank you, son, for understanding. But hey, with any luck at all I won't have to go anywhere. Coop's surely on his way home by now."

"Yeah," Wes said. "But, Dad . . . ? If you do have to go, you won't need to worry about us. You can count on me."

The lump that rose that time in Morgan's throat kept him silent until they got back to the shed.

Morgan had to stifle a groan when he swung down from the saddle. He wasn't sore yet. The groan was in anticipation of the aches he knew he'd have the next day. It had been a long time since he'd ridden. Too long.

"I'll be dead tomorrow," he complained. "Whose idea was this, anyway?"

Wes pulled the saddle from his black gelding and set it on the waiting sawhorse. Laughing, he said, "Yours."

They put the tack away in the tackroom at the back of the shed and cooled and groomed the horses. When they finished, Wes headed for the house at a lope.

"There's at least a gallon of iced tea in the fridge with my name on it. You comin', Dad?"

"You go ahead. I'll be along in a while."

Iced tea sounded great, but Morgan had just seen Sarah enter the chicken house. He was drawn to her like one of her hens was drawn to a roost.

Before he reached the building he heard Sarah cry out.

"Ouch! Damn you, Cogburn!'

There followed a loud squawking, then a cloud of heavy dust billowed out the open door.

"I've always said that at your age you were too tough to eat, but I bet if I stewed you for a couple of days and threw in a mess of dumplings, nobody'd complain. Ouch! Stop that!"

Morgan leaned against the frame of the open door and watched Sarah do a quick two-step with a big white rooster who was flapping his wings at her.

"I've heard of people talking to their animals, but you hold entire conversations."

Sarah whirled at the sound of his voice, and Morgan broke out laughing. She wore her usual garb of T-shirt and jeans, the latter tucked into a pair of calf-high rubber boots. According to her, rubber was better, because you didn't have to worry about what you stepped in, and you could just hose them off. Her hair was stuffed up inside a green ball cap bearing a yellow John Deere logo.

It was the bandana that set him off. She had it tied around her head so it covered her face from just below her eyes down. "You gonna rob a bank, or just steal some eggs?"

"Real funny, Foster." She tugged the bandana down until it lay in loose folds around her neck. The lower half of her face was clean. The top definitely was not. "Actually, it's a breathing filter. I'm cleaning out in here. You won't want to stay without one of your own."

"What was all the hollering about just now?"

"Nothing serious. I was just going another round with Cogburn."

"Who?"

"Cogburn," she said, waving toward the white rooster. "Rooster Cogburn."

Morgan groaned and rolled his eyes. A mare named Spot, a cow named Edna, and now this. "Okay, I give up. Why did you name him Rooster Cogburn?"

"Are you kidding? Look at him. He's old, he's scruffy, he's mean as a junk-yard dog, he's tough as old shoe leather, and he's only got one eye. What would you name him?"

He shook his head. "John Wayne must be rolling in his grave."

"I doubt it. He's probably proud."

Sarah bent down, her back to Cogburn, and reached for the broom lying at her feet. The rooster in question executed a quick series of intricate dance steps—Morgan could have sworn he saw a peculiar glint in that one orange eye—then flapped his wings twice. In the next instant the bird leaped into the air, stuck his feet out in front of him, and jabbed Sarah right in the rear with a set of wicked-looking two-inch spurs growing from the inside of his legs just above his feet.

Sarah shrieked and bolted upright like a loaded spring. She whirled to face her attacker with blood—or chicken and dumplings—in her eyes. "Git!"

Morgan nearly doubled over with laughter. Cogburn arched his neck up and let out a triumphant crow. Then, after ruffling his feathers, he cast Sarah what could only be described as a disdainful look from that one orange eye. As regal as any other reigning monarch, the bird strutted slowly past Sarah and Morgan and out the door.

Sarah shook her fist in the air. "One of these days," she muttered.

"You're all talk."

With a self-deprecating grin she said, "Yeah, I know. But he's been around here so long he's like part of the place. I just can't bring myself to wring his neck. How was your ride?"

"Fine."

She cocked her head to one side. "Did you want something?"

Morgan grinned. "Now there's a loaded question if I ever heard one."

Sarah smirked. "Now who's all talk?"

"What's that supposed to mean?" As soon as the words were out he wanted them back. It was a dumb question. He knew exactly what she meant. This wasn't the kind of conversation he wanted to deal with just then.

How could he explain to her that talk was not all he wanted? She stirred something in him that had never been stirred before. He'd never wanted a woman with this much . . . intensity.

But he'd never trusted a woman less in his life. How could he be sure she wasn't using the bait of her body simply to keep him from taking the kids?

"Oh, I see," she said, her hands on her hips. "It's your intention then just to tease me to death."

Morgan forced himself to relax. So what if she was only using him? He'd never intended to make her any promises. Why couldn't they have a good time together and just see what developed? If he felt used, he could always leave.

But could you, buddy? Could you leave her?

That was the problem. He didn't know. And he feared it was already too late for him anyway. He should have left days ago.

So why are you fighting her? She wants you as much as you want her.

And why couldn't he trust her? Sarah wasn't the type of woman for deceit. She was too open, too honest. It was there in her face, in those intriguing eyes.

"Tease you to death? Is that what you think?"

Her eyes were suddenly serious. "What else am I supposed to think? Why else do you put a convenient distance between us whenever the children aren't around to chaperon?"

"I outgrew needing a chaperon years ago."

"Couldn't prove it by me."

He felt a slow grin spread across his face. Somewhere between her last sentence and his, he'd surrendered. Hell, he couldn't fight both of them. "You're gonna eat those words, lady."

She grinned back at him. "Promises, promises."

SIX

Sarah let the spray of the shower wash away the day's grime. The kids and Morgan were watching television and she planned to join them. But first she wanted to be clean. What she'd really like to do was put on something nice for a change, rather than jeans.

But if she walked into the living room in anything other than jeans, the kids would comment. She *never* wore anything but jeans and T-shirts around the house. *Damnit.*

Well, she thought, toweling her hair dry, she could at least put on a little makeup and perfume. She picked up the bottle that read, in bold red slashes, Entice.

"Yeah, Entice." Good name. Good idea. But just so she wouldn't be too obvious, she only put on a dab here and there. Mustn't forget there.

When she entered the living room a few minutes later, she took the vacant spot on the couch next to Angie, who sat beside Morgan. Angie still rarely spoke to him, but at least she'd stopped shying away every time he got near. And she didn't mind when he touched her.

Sarah could understand that. *She* didn't mind when he touched *her*, either. She tried to concentrate on the Disney movie the kids were so absorbed in, and halfway succeeded.

Then Morgan yawned and stretched and draped his arm along the back of the couch. A moment later she felt his fingers in her hair. She glanced at him, but his gaze was trained on the television. A moment later she nearly moaned aloud when he stroked the side of her neck with one calloused finger. Goose bumps raced down her arms. She tried to rub them away.

"Cold?"

She turned toward the low sound of his voice. His hand cupped the back of her neck as their gazes met and held. "No," she whispered. *Not on your life.*

He smiled a slow, sensual smile as though he'd read her thoughts.

An instant later the spell was broken when Angie flopped her head in Sarah's lap and her feet in Morgan's.

After the movie, Sarah puttered in the kitchen for a few minutes to give the kids time to get in bed. When she went up to tell them good night, Morgan was right behind her. He followed her back downstairs.

Now what was she supposed to do?

She stopped in the middle of the darkened living room. He stopped, too, mere inches behind her.

She could feel the heat from his body, hear his breathing. Her heart raced in anticipation.

"I hope you've got one of those left for me."

His deep voice sent waves of awareness and longing washing over her. "One of those what?"

He took her hand and turned her toward him. "One of those good-night kisses."

This was it then. The moment she'd been waiting for all day. All her life. If he wasn't going to kiss her, she was sure enough going to kiss him. "I might have one left over. Or two."

She glided into his arms. It was where she was meant to be. When their lips met, there was nothing slow or tentative about it. It was as if they were starved for the taste and touch of each other. Their tongues danced an erotic duet. Their bodies swayed to their own inner music.

Morgan groaned and tore his mouth away. He felt his control slipping and buried his face against her hair. "Sarah, Sarah, you smell so good. I don't remember when I've smelled anything as good as you."

"It's my perfume." She was planting little nibbling kisses along his chest through his shirt and doing things with her hands on his back that drove him wild. "It's called Entice."

He nuzzled against her temple until she raised her lips to meet his once more. "It certainly does that," he said with feeling.

As their lips met, he pulled her even closer until she was pressed firmly against his body. She surely couldn't help but feel his arousal. Things were moving fast. Too fast. He had to stop. He knew he had to stop.

He tore his lips from hers and gasped for breath. "Sweet, sweet Sarah, I'm rushing you, I know it. I don't want to rush you."

She pulled his head down to hers again. Against his lips she whispered, "Rush me, Morgan. Rush me."

Sarah had no idea where the bold words came from, but she was glad for them. She wanted him, had wanted him for days and days. And he wanted her. She could tell by the way he groaned and thrust his tongue into her mouth.

Then suddenly he was pulling away. Again. "No, don't leave."

His breathing was as heavy and strained as hers when he asked, "Are you sure, Sarah?''"

Her laugh sounded husky and provocative, even to her. "I'm sure." She looked up into his shadowed face. "I've never had to ask a man to make love before. Do I have to ask you, Morgan?"

He took a sharp breath, held it, then let it out with a grin. "But will you still respect me in the morning?"

She smoothed a fingertip over his wet lips. "If the night is even half what I expect it to be, I'll probably worship the ground you walk on."

"I'll do my best not to disappoint you."

"The only way you could disappoint me would be by making me spend another night alone."

A growling sound came from deep within Morgan's throat. He kissed her hard and quick. "Not on your life." He swept her up in his arms and carried her into her bedroom. There he placed her gently on the bed and stood beside it.

When he started unbuttoning his shirt, Sarah knelt on the bed and brushed his hands away. "Let me." Eager for the feel of his smooth, muscled chest, she ignored the trembling of her fingers. She purposely refrained from touching his skin while she slipped the buttons from their holes. When they were all undone, she swept the shirt off his shoulders and down his arms and let it fall to the floor.

And then she touched him. She placed her hands flat against his stomach and felt him suck in a sharp breath. A heady sense of power surged through her. With her fingers spread wide, she stroked him, slowly, from the waistband of his jeans up, up over the smooth, muscled contours of his glorious chest, up to his shoulders, then slowly, slowly back down again.

She'd never been so bold with a man before. She'd never been so intimate with a man she'd known only a couple of weeks. But none of that seemed to matter. It felt so right to be touching him this way. Tremors of excitement streaked from where her fingers met his satiny skin to the tips of her toes. It was like nothing she'd ever experienced before.

Morgan thought he might die from her touch, but he didn't care. Such a simple thing, fingers on skin, yet such complicated, exotic, erotic feelings. He was dying, and he didn't care. He'd fought for his life every day for the past four years, just so he could die from pleasure at her touch. So long as she kept touching him and touching him and, oh God, now she was kissing his chest.

He'd known her touch would do this to him. He'd never reached the edge of his endurance so fast before, but he'd known it would happen with her.

"My turn." He pulled her hands away and raised her arms over her head, then peeled her T-shirt up and off. After locating the hooks on her bra, he released them and tossed the offending garment aside . . . then sucked in his breath. Her breasts were small and perfect and pale in the shadowed room. Her nipples were already hard. He stroked one with his thumb and she gasped.

Slowly, so as to savor every delicious, agonizing second, he pressed her against his chest.

At the contact, they both moaned. Morgan felt the strength leave his knees. He kissed her then.

It was such a tender, soulful kiss, Sarah felt tears form behind her closed lids. She leaned back on the bed and he came with her. The kiss grew more heated by the second, until she could feel his desperation, his consuming hunger. And it became her hunger.

When their legs entwined, she didn't even wonder where their jeans had gone, she was only glad they'd disappeared. His hands were everywhere, and she couldn't get enough of his touch, or of touching him.

"Sarah, Sarah, Sarah . . ." He trailed searing kisses down her throat to first one nipple, then the other. He licked, he tugged, he suckled, and he drove her wild with wanting him. She gasped and writhed beneath him, urging him on with her movements, urging him to fill the empty, aching void he'd created the first time he shook her hand. She wanted him in her life, in her body. He was already in her heart.

He cupped his hand over the dark curls between her thighs and felt her hips rush up to meet his questing fingers. She was tight and hot and ready. Her response to his touch, her thrusting hips, and the little whimpering sounds coming from her throat were making him crazy. Never had a woman's response filled him with such awe, such a sense of elation and power.

When he rolled on top of her, she cradled him with her thighs. "Morgan, please . . ."

"Yes. Yes!"

He entered her part way, then withdrew. Entered, withdrew. Until he was fully sheathed in her hot, silken depths. There he paused. Nothing in life had ever felt so perfect. Never had he known such a feeling of home, of peace.

Peace. A strange word considering the throbbing ache in his loins and the fierce pounding of his heart.

He wanted to savor the sensation, to draw it out. But Sarah had other ideas. She moved beneath him and suddenly he couldn't wait another moment. He answered her movement with an ever-increasing rhythm that echoed in his blood like the beat of a thousand primitive drums.

Higher and higher, faster and faster they flew, until a million tiny stars burst and showered them with the miracle of release.

As Morgan gave a last forceful shudder, he heard the words from her sweet, sweet lips, the words his empty soul had unknowingly been thirsting for. Words that both thrilled and terrified him.

"I love you," she said.

Later, when his mind again began to function and his breathing calmed, he realized she couldn't have meant it. She barely knew him. She'd been married for years. Saying "I love you" after making love was probably a habit, something she'd always said to her husband.

He swallowed, and the taste in his mouth was suddenly bitter. He didn't like to think of her with a husband. To block the thought from his mind and hers, he kissed her again, and was astounded when desire shot through him every bit as powerful as it had been earlier. She melted into his arms as though they hadn't made love in years, rather than mere minutes.

Morgan came awake slowly, savoring the soft warmth draped across him. There was no moment of confusion, no doubt as to where he was. He was in Sarah's bed, in Sarah's arms. Her head rested against his heart. Right where it belonged.

He stared up at the ceiling, a gray blur in the dark room, trying to remember the last time he'd awakened with a woman at his side. It had to have been sometime—a long time—before his divorce.

God, but he'd never felt such sheer contentment, such peace, in his life as he had this past night.

His misgivings, his doubts about Sarah's motives, his fear that she was using him to keep the children, had been burned to a cinder in the heat of their passion. She belonged to him now. And he belonged to her, the way he'd never belonged anywhere in his life before.

Something tickled his chest. He smiled. It was her eyelashes. "You're awake," he whispered.

"Hmm," she moaned as she stretched against him. She snuggled her head into the hollow of his shoulder and rubbed her leg the length of his. His pulse quickened. "Is it morning?"

Her slender, supple fingers brushed across his nipple. His breath quickened. "Close enough," he managed. "I should go, before the kids wake up."

She raised her head, and even in the dim glow from the yard light, he could see the blue in her eyes, eyes that had once been gray. She smiled at him with lips still puffy from his kisses more than two hours ago. "Not yet," she whispered. Her mouth lowered to his. "I want you to take my breath away. Again."

His blood quickened.

Morgan stepped out of the shower and toweled off, whistling all the while. Whistling was the only release he allowed himself. What he really wanted to do was throw back his head and laugh out loud with sheer, unadulterated delight.

He had taken her breath away, just as Sarah had taken his. By all rights he should be exhausted, what with all the unaccustomed activity and lack of sleep. Instead, he felt exhilarated. Like he could conquer the world. There were a few muscles that ached, he thought with a grin, but it was a pleasant ache.

He wrapped the towel around his hips and opened the bathroom door.

"Hiya, Dad. How's those sore muscles?"

Morgan's head snapped up. Wes was coming down the stairs, a bounce in his step and laughter in his eyes. Morgan, his mind a sudden blank, unbelievably felt his face heat up. He swallowed. "Uh . . . huh?"

"Muscles," Wes said. "You know, as in all that unaccustomed activity?"

Morgan blinked, trying to orient himself. "Uh . . . activity?"

"Yeah, like riding?"

A sudden picture of the *ride* or two (or three!) he'd taken last night flashed across his mind. The heat in his face increased. *Good God, I'm blushing!*

"Horseback riding?" Wes prodded.

Horseback riding! Morgan fought the relieved laughter threatening to choke him. "Right. Horseback riding. No problem."

Wes and Morgan were the last two to reach the breakfast table. The first thing Morgan noticed was that Sarah wasn't wearing a bra. It was the first time she'd gone without one since his second day here.

His eyes darted up to hers, and he fought a smile. He also fought a groan. The mere thought of her unbound breasts was enough to make him ache. He remembered the feel of them in his hands, the taste of them on his lips. The way she gasped and moaned when he—

He had to stop such thoughts or he'd never be able to get up from the table. He tore his gaze from hers but made the mistake of glancing once more at the front of her T-shirt. At the sight of her hardened nipples practically poking holes in the fabric, he sucked in his breath and looked away.

Sarah felt the blush sting her cheeks as her nipples hardened beneath his heated gaze. Good Lord! Was that all it took from him? One look? She was on fire with wanting him again. After the night they'd just spent, she'd have thought it impossible to feel such desire so soon.

But she'd been wrong.

Morgan glanced sharply at Wes, but the boy was too busy eating to notice anything but the food on his plate. The same was true of the rest of the children.

"I own that one!' Jeff cried. "That's fifty dollars you owe me. Pay up, bud."

Rob groaned and tossed the required sum across the Monopoly board to Jeff.

From where she stood at the sink, Sarah grinned at their play. She'd been relieved when the children had decided to play Monopoly. She preferred they play indoors when it was this hot outside. The upper-ninety-degree temperatures of the past few days were usually reserved for August. The heat, and apparently the drought, had hit a few weeks early this year.

She peeled back the husk and tried to get as much of the silk as possible off the last ear of corn. And it was literally the last ear. The last ear she'd picked this morning; the last ear of the season.

Suddenly she felt a heated presence at her back. *Morgan.* She knew it was Morgan without even looking. It was like having a field of supercharged electrical energy swoop down on her, making every nerve in her body go on alert.

He leaned around her shoulder, so close she felt his breath on her cheek, and blocked her view of the children at the kitchen table. "I thought you finished canning that corn an hour ago." His smile caused her pulse to leap.

Then he touched her. His hand brushed up her left side, where the children couldn't see. Up her ribs. With one finger he traced the outer curve of her breast.

"I'm . . . uh . . ."

"Yes?"

Sarah swallowed. He was driving her crazy, touching her this way, gazing at her with his hot brown eyes, right there in the same room with the children. And he was doing it on purpose. She smiled at him slowly.

"I did finish the canning. These ears are for supper."

He traced a line along the undercurve of her breast. She felt her nipples tighten. She was breathing heavy now.

"I thought corn was supposed to follow that old saying, 'knee-high by the Fourth of July.' But yours was already over your head by then."

What was he talking about? Oh yeah, corn. How could he talk about corn when his hand was

. . . oh, his hand! She tried to still the trembling in her knees, but couldn't. "Our . . . uh . . . season starts earlier . . . this far south."

"What else are we having for dinner besides corn?" His voice was low and calm, but she felt his rapid heartbeat against her right arm.

"Nothing, if you don't stop that," she whispered, fighting a grin.

That finger of his raced up and flipped across her nipple, bringing it and its mate to sharp points beneath her T-shirt. She gasped and accidentally jabbed her thumbnail into a plump kernel. Milky white juice squirted over her hand. "Look what you made me do."

"It's what you get," he said, his voice strained, his eyes on the front of her shirt, "for running around half dressed." He grinned wickedly, then abruptly turned away and joined the kids at the kitchen table.

Sarah sagged against the sink and turned the water on full blast to cover the sound of her harsh breathing. With her back to the others, she allowed her own grin to blossom. The dirty rotten scoundrel. She'd get him for that.

The next few days were the most glorious of Sarah's life. And the nights were unbelievable. She and Morgan took and gave and loved and laughed. She saw a side of him she'd never seen before—a young, carefree, happy side.

He eased up on his sexual teasing during the days, and she grew more comfortable around him than she remembered being with anyone else in the past.

The only dark spot was when he crept from her bed like a thief in the night just before dawn each morning. She knew why he did it. It wouldn't do for the children to find them in bed together. But still it tore her apart to let him go each morning.

"Don't you ever get tired of cooking for this crew?" Morgan asked.

Sarah paused in the act of opening a package of noodles. "Do I hear an offer in there somewhere?"

Morgan grinned. "I just realized it's been nearly five years since I've had pizza. What do you say we load everybody in the car and eat out?"

Sarah leaned back against the cabinet and answered his grin. "What's the matter? Did you finally notice your name on tonight's KP list?"

"You wound me," he protested. "I just thought you might enjoy a night away from the stove. A trip to town. Don't you like pizza?"

Rob poked his head in the door. "Did somebody say pizza?"

Connie was right behind him. "Did somebody say town?"

A half hour later the seven of them were seated around a large table at the pizza place in Prague.

"There you are, you devils, you. I've been wondering why I hadn't seen y'all in town."

Sarah had to force herself to keep from cringing. She plastered a smile on her face and turned to greet Myrna Selznick, bank teller and gossip extraordinaire, and her husband, Otto.

"My, what a lovely family. I've always said that, haven't I, Otto? But now, with Mr. Foster here, why it's just downright perfect. Don't you think so, Otto?"

Perfect. Yes, as far as Sarah was concerned, life was as close to perfect as it could get.

Friday evening the whole family drove back to Chandler, this time to watch Rita barrel race at the local rodeo. The small arena was near Tilghman Park where the July Fourth activities had been held, separated from it only by the Chandler Lions football stadium.

Ben and Kenny Hudspeth waved as they dashed after their parents, who were leading Rita's horse toward the far end of the arena where the starting chutes were located. The family waved back and wished Rita good luck.

Family. In every sense but one, they were a real family, and Sarah refused to think beyond the here and now.

Morgan's thoughts were similar as he herded the kids up into the bleachers beside the arena. They felt like a real family. But unlike Sarah, he did look toward the future. Would this last? Could they make it work?

In the last few days, Sarah had withheld nothing from him. She was a warm, giving woman who filled his days with wonder and his nights with fiery passion. She made him feel loved and wanted. She made him feel . . . important. Important to her. It had to be real.

"Howdy, neighbors," Barry called. He climbed the bleachers and joined them.

"Shouldn't you be with Rita?" Sarah asked. "They'll be running the barrels soon."

Barry grinned. "She ran me off. I made the mistake of giving her some last-minute advice on when to lean and when to rein. She threatened to take her crop to me."

Ben and Kenny joined them next, each carrying a hot dog and soft drink. That, of course, sparked a string of requests from his own children, and Morgan soon found himself digging into his pocket to spring for a trip to the concession stand.

"Gee thanks, Dad," Wes said with a grin.

Sarah leaned toward Morgan and laughed. "Sucker."

"Yeah, Dad, thanks," Connie and Rob and Jeff threw over their shoulders as they clambered down the bleachers.

Angie didn't say anything, but she stopped halfway down and gave Morgan a shy little smile.

"So how's things at the Collins place these days?" Barry asked. "You gonna be sticking around awhile, Foster?"

"Oh, look," Sarah said, grateful to change the subject. "They're setting up the barrels."

"Just how do you race barrels, anyway?" Morgan asked, trying to avoid thinking about Barry's question, and how fast Sarah had changed the subject.

"You're kidding, right?"

"I don't think he's kidding, Barry."

"Of course I'm not kidding. This isn't exactly

an everyday occurrence where I'm from. What do you do, line them up in a row and shout 'go?' "

Barry rolled his eyes and groaned while Sarah snickered.

After controlling her laughter, Sarah took on a grave, lecturing tone. "I feel compelled, sir, to correct your misconception. The barrels themselves do not race. The riders race *around* the barrels."

The kids came back talking and laughing and balancing food as they climbed the bleachers. Wes carried Angie's for her because she had to use both hands to negotiate the climb. She wormed her way between Sarah and Morgan, and once she had her food, settled down to eat.

A moment later Morgan felt a slight tug on his shirt sleeve. He turned and looked down into the giant, guileless eyes of his youngest child. She had mustard and chili smeared from ear to ear and fingertips to elbows. "Hi, there," he said, smiling.

Timidly, she answered his smile. Then she held up her partially eaten hot dog. A glob of chili oozed out and plopped onto the seat between them. "Want some?"

Morgan was elated. He could count the number of times she'd spoken to him on the fingers of one hand. But for a child who ate like there was no tomorrow, to offer him part of her food was a major breakthrough. His eyes misted over. They were going to make it. They were going to become a real family, and Angie was going to eventually accept him as her father. His heart swelled and threatened to cut off his breath as he accepted the bite she offered.

"Here comes Mom," one of the Hudspeth boys called.

The children quieted, and along with the three adults in the group, leaned forward and cheered as Rita and her horse shot out of the gate.

It looked deceptively easy to Morgan, to ride out and circle the three barrels in a cloverleaf pattern, but he knew it wasn't. Rita's time of sixteen point nine seconds was announced over the loudspeaker. The crowd roared with approval.

"That's my girl!" Barry shouted. He and his boys left to go congratulate Rita on the fastest time of the night so far, and to cool down her horse for her.

By the time the last barrel racer was finished, no one had beaten Rita's time. Three had come close, with times ranging from seventeen to seventeen and a half seconds, but that still left Rita the winner.

While a crew removed the barrels and set up for something called "pole bending," Morgan decided he was hungry. He could still taste that bite of Angie's hot dog—the first hot dog he'd had in over four years—and it tasted damn good.

All five kids decided they should go with him and help him find his way to the concession stand. Sarah laughed and said she'd stay where she was. "You're being suckered in again."

Morgan returned her laugh, and on impulse did something he'd never done in public before. He kissed her. Right in front of the kids. Just a brief peck on the nose, but it was enough to make her blush.

While Morgan stopped at the bottom of the bleachers to congratulate Rita, Sarah tried to still the pounding of her heart. He'd never kissed her in front of the children before, much less in front of dozens of strangers.

A minute later, a hot, tired, but exhilarated Rita flopped down next to her. "That man is an absolute hunk."

Sarah smiled at her best friend. "He is, isn't he?"

Morgan stopped halfway to the concession stand and realized he hadn't asked Sarah what she wanted to eat. The kids went on ahead of him and he turned back. When he crossed behind the bleachers directly beneath where Sarah and Rita sat on the top row, their conversation stopped him cold.

". . . and I say you're a fool if you let him take those kids away from you. We both know how much you love them. Baby him, mother him, pamper him. Hell, sleep with him. But don't let him take those kids."

"I'm doing my best, Rita, believe me."

Morgan failed to hear the rest of Sarah's answer due to the sudden buzzing in his ears. His guts twisted into a painful knot. His heart constricted, and something within him turned cold and died.

She was using him. All her soft sighs and I-love-yous, her searing kisses and passionate lovemaking were nothing more than a ruse to keep him from leaving with the most important thing in her life—his children.

He should have known. He *had* known. Only

he'd talked himself into believing otherwise. He felt betrayed, and he'd never known betrayal could hurt so much. He'd believed in her. He'd cared for her. He'd . . . yes, damnit, he'd loved her.

The hell of it was, he still loved her, even knowing what he did. So what was he going to do about it?

Sarah didn't think too much about Morgan's silence on the way home. But when she woke the next morning to realize she'd spent the night alone, she knew something was wrong. As soon as the children scattered to their various pursuits after breakfast, she followed Morgan to the office and barely prevented having the door shut in her face.

"Oh, sorry," he said. "Didn't know you were behind me."

Then, as if he'd never kissed her, never held her in his arms, never made sweet, tormenting love to her and whispered hot, sultry words in the dark, he turned his back, sat down at her late husband's desk, and turned on the computer.

Sarah was hurt and confused. And suddenly very unsure of herself and afraid to broach the topic she'd meant to discuss. "How's the . . . uh . . . report coming?"

"Not too bad."

She stared longingly at the way the muscles in his back and shoulders flexed as he typed in the name of a document to call it up to the screen.

What was wrong? What had happened to turn him back into a cold, forbidding stranger? "Can I get you anything?"

He tossed a careless smile over his shoulder, then turned back to the computer screen. "No thanks. Breakfast was great. I don't need anything else for a while."

"Morgan?"

"Hmm?" The rhythmic clacking of the keyboard never ceased as he spoke.

"Is . . . something wrong?"

"Not a thing that I can think of."

Then why didn't you come to me last night? she wanted to ask. But she didn't. Instead, she turned chicken and fled, closing the office door behind her.

She would have plucked up her courage and tried again, but Morgan made certain the two of them were never alone by keeping at least two children with him at all times.

When he didn't come to her room again that night, she could have gone to his, but she didn't. Something had obviously happened to change his mind. He'd had second thoughts about his involvement with her.

Maybe he was used to more exciting women. Maybe he was bored with her. Whatever, it was clear he didn't want to talk about it, whatever *it* was.

Three nights in a row she lay in bed yearning for his warmth beside her, longing for his touch, his kiss. His companionship. How had she come to so totally depend on him for her happiness? How had she let it happen?

The days weren't any better. The weather turned

viciously hot. All the children stayed indoors most of the time, savoring the central air-conditioning. No one went out into the one-hundred-degree-plus heat—(with ninety percent humidity!)—unless they had to.

At morning and evening chore times, they had to. The evening after the rodeo, Angie ran screaming and sobbing to Sarah.

"What is it, Angie? What's wrong?" Sarah asked.

Morgan came and knelt beside his daughter, but the girl wouldn't look at him. She hugged Sarah's legs. The soul-shattering sobs tore at Sarah's heart. "What is it, sweetie?" she asked again.

"He's g-gone," Angie sobbed.

Morgan smoothed Angie's hair back from her face. The sight of that big, dark hand so tenderly stroking the small child nearly brought Sarah to her knees.

But she couldn't think about Morgan now. Angie needed her. "Who's gone?" she asked.

"Speedy Turtle!" Angie wailed. "I went to give him water, an' he was g-gone!"

Morgan put his hand on Angie's shoulder and tried to turn her around. She clung to Sarah all the harder. "Come on, Angie," he said softly. "I'll help you look for him."

"No! He's all g-gone. I don't want you, I want Sarah."

Morgan's face hardened. When he looked up at Sarah she saw frustration and anger mixed with pain glittering in his dark eyes. "She didn't mean anything by it, Morgan, she's just upset.'' But even as she spoke, she realized his anger wasn't directed at Angie, but at her.

What? she wanted to scream. *What have I done?*

Even though she knew it was useless, Sarah went through the motions of looking for Speedy, with Angie clinging to her legs the whole time. The turtle was gone.

When they went back to the house, it took another half hour for Sarah to calm the child. Angie was so exhausted from the emotional upheaval that she fell asleep in Sarah's lap on the couch.

Before Sarah could get up with her precious burden, Morgan scooped the child out of her arms. ''I'll put her to bed,'' he said tersely. The look in his eyes warned Sarah against protesting.

She went to bed early that night and spent another night alone.

Rita phoned the next day. ''So how goes the campaign?''

''The what?'' Sarah asked.

''You know. The campaign to keep that gorgeous hunk and his kids from leaving the farm? How goes it?''

Sarah wanted to cry. She wanted to hang up the phone. She wanted to run and hide. But most of all, she wanted Morgan. ''I . . . uh . . . can't talk right now, Rita.''

''You all right, kid? You sound kinda funny.''

''I'm . . . all right.''

In the office, Morgan stared at the receiver in his hand as though it were responsible for all the world's evils. Gently, he forced himself to hang up. What he really wanted to do was throw the offending instrument across the room.

He'd been so engrossed in his report, he hadn't realized the phone had rung. He'd picked it up intending to call Benson and check on Coop. Instead, he got Sarah and Rita.

Damn her! So he was a campaign, was he? A project. Prevent forest fires. Save the whales. *Keep the children.*

Damn her!

What a lie, Sarah thought after hanging up the kitchen phone. She'd told Rita she was all right, when she'd never been less all right in her life.

If it weren't so damned hot outside she'd take Spot and ride until she was ready to drop. It would get her out of the house, away from Morgan.

Not that she saw much of him. But just being in the same house with him hurt. She could feel his coldness, his . . . hostility. Yes, that's what it was. Hostility. But why?

He was going to leave soon, she knew. The only thing she didn't understand, aside from why he'd suddenly pulled away from her, was why, after three nights and two days of maintaining a sometimes polite, sometimes hostile, but always cool distance, why was he still here at all?

Morgan was asking himself the same question. Why was he still there? Why hadn't he packed up the kids and left the morning after the rodeo? The rodeo, where his worst fears had been confirmed.

But he knew why, and the reason was enough to make him sick. He still wanted her. No matter that she was only using him to keep the children, he still wanted her. He wanted her laughter, her smiles, her touch, her kiss. He wanted that exquisite sensation he could find nowhere on earth but in her arms, with his body buried deep inside hers.

Yet he refused to let himself be used.

He had no choice. If he was to retain any ounce of pride and self-respect at all, he had to leave and leave soon. If he stayed around much longer, he could easily end up groveling at her feet.

Isn't a woman like Sarah worth a grovel or two, ol' buddy?

Not if she didn't love him.

Morgan hit the Save button on the computer, then picked up the phone again, making certain he had a dial tone, and called Benson.

When he learned there was still no word on Coop, he again wanted to throw the phone across the room. This time he settled for slamming the receive into the cradle.

If he didn't get out of that room, he'd go crazy. When he turned off the computer he could hear the television in the living room. Good. That meant the kids were in the house.

It was a relief to open the office door and get out for a while. He headed for the living room, intent on finding his cover—two or more children.

Wes was the only one in the living room, and he was just turning off the television when Morgan walked in. Morgan tried to make small talk, but Wes had other ideas.

"You and Sarah have a fight?"

Morgan stared at Wes, dismayed. Here was another question he should have anticipated but hadn't. There'd been enough tension in the air between him and Sarah lately, there was no way the kids wouldn't have noticed. But still, he wasn't ready to admit anything. "What makes you ask that?"

Wes shrugged and turned to look out the front window. "I just wondered, since you're not sleeping with her anymore."

SEVEN

A slight breeze could have knocked Morgan flat. He felt like an invisible fist had just slammed into his chest. Embarrassment was the first thing he felt, when he could feel again. Then, anger. Unreasonable anger. With himself, for not being strong enough to stay away from Sarah in the first place. With Sarah for deceiving him. And finally, with Wes.

"Don't you ever let me hear you talking about Sarah like that again," he warned.

"Me?" Wes spun around, outrage clearly etched on his face. "*Me?* You're the one who sleeps with her one night, then treats her like she's got the plague."

"That's enough! What Sarah and I do or don't do is none of your business. I don't ever want to hear another word out of you about it."

"Yes, sir!" Wes accompanied his sarcastic remark with an equally sarcastic salute, then spun on his heel and stormed out of the room.

For the third time in less than an hour, Morgan

wanted to throw something. Or better yet, hit something. How could he have let this happen? Damn, but he'd been stupid. And not just in how he'd handled Wes, but from the very beginning.

It was time to get out. Now.

He went looking for the rest of the kids. He made it through the house without running into Sarah, but his luck ran out in the backyard. There she stood, looking hot and every bit as frustrated as he felt, and not a kid in sight to keep her from demanding an explanation for his recent behavior.

It wasn't even ten o'clock yet, but the giant thermometer on the back porch had read ninety when he'd passed it. He'd been outside mere seconds and could already feel sweat trickling down his spine. Yet the ice chips in Sarah's gray eyes were enough to make him shiver.

She stood there, so cool-looking in her faded, skintight jeans and breast-hugging T-shirt, arms crossed, one booted toe tapping on the ground like an impatient schoolteacher. With raised brows she said, "You're alone."

He resented her coolness in the stifling heat. He resented . . . hell, he resented *her*. Her and her lies. If she hadn't batted those big eyes at him, hadn't twitched that damned rear of hers, he'd never have been tempted to fall into her trap. If she hadn't decided she wanted to keep the children—*his* children, children who didn't belong to her—none of this would have happened. That scene a minute ago with Wes would never have taken place.

His defenses rose. He was through blaming himself for what was her fault. "Where are the kids?"

"Here and there. You're avoiding me. I'd like to know why."

"Am I?"

"Am I?" she mimicked.

His hackles rose. She'd sent the kids off somewhere and laid in wait for him. Ambushed him. He could read the truth in her eyes. Damn. Now what?

Now what? were Sarah's exact thoughts, too. Now that she had him, what was she going to do with him? The more she thought about the way he'd withdrawn from her without a word of explanation, the madder she got. She'd never been dumped by a man before, but if this was it, she didn't care for the feeling.

"I think I deserve an explanation," she said, struggling to keep the hurt and anger from her voice.

Morgan shrugged and looked away. "What kind of explanation would you like?"

"How about the truth?"

"About what?"

She ground her teeth together to keep from screaming at him. Tears stung the backs of her eyes. "You know about what."

He looked at her then, his eyes dark and emotionless. "You mean about why I quit availing myself of your . . . services?"

Sarah gasped. By the time he finished speaking, his eyes were no longer emotionless, they were filled with contempt. Bile rose in her throat.

"What kind of fool do you take me for?" he said with a sneer. "Did you honestly think I was so blind I couldn't see what you were doing?"

"What are you talking about?"

"Oh, that's good. That look of innocence. Do you practice it in front of the mirror? It's damn good, I'll give you that. Must have taken you years to perfect it."

Stunned by his outburst, Sarah took a step away from him. Had he gone crazy? She repeated her question. "What are you talking about?"

"Fear? Oh that's even better. Just the right touch of fear mixed in with the innocence. You are good, honey. But it won't work."

His dark eyes bored into hers and a shiver of apprehension shot up her spine. "Morgan—"

"Did you think I didn't understand how desperate you were to keep me from taking my children away from you? Did you think I didn't know why you lured me into your bed?"

"Lured! That's the most—"

"And you thought you had me, didn't you? You thought after four years on the run in the jungle, with no women to speak of, I'd be so desperate for the crumbs of your affection I'd close my eyes to what you really wanted and let you lead me around on a leash."

"How dare you say that!"

"Oh, I dare, all right."

"You actually think I'm capable of something like that?"

"I do. You forget, deceit is part of my profession. It's been my job for years to practice it and uncover it. I finally got sick of it in my job, so I quit. I'll be damned if I'll stand for it in my private life."

Sarah couldn't believe this was happening. She hadn't known what to expect from him, but this . . . "You really think I . . . we . . . made love—"

"Call it what it was, Sarah. It wasn't love, it was sex, plain ol' everyday, run-of-the-mill sex."

Sarah reeled as though she'd been struck. *Run-of-the-mill sex.*

Then she straightened, and every ounce of emotion seemed to drain right out of her. She felt nothing. Nothing but a cold, hard emptiness. She stared at him without really seeing him. He was just a figure standing before her, nothing more. He meant nothing. She meant nothing. "If I was . . . using you, what were you doing?"

"The same," he said calmly. "Using you. I needed a place to stay for the kids and myself until I figured out what I wanted to do, where I wanted to go. Here was as good a place as any, better than some. And despite what I may think of you, you are a good cook. The food alone was worth the trouble."

Her eyes widened with every word he spoke. The coldness within her turned to red hot rage. How could she possibly have thought she was in love with such a cruel, calculating bastard. She glared her hatred at him. "And have you figured it out—where to go?"

"Just about."

"Good," she said, clenching her fists to keep from scratching his eyes out. "So you'll be leaving soon."

"Yeah."

"We have a saying around here, Morgan."

"What's that?"

She narrowed her eyes to an angry squint. " 'Don't let the door hit you in the ass.' "

She turned, intending to stalk off, but he grabbed her arm. "What's that supposed to mean?"

"It means, Mr. Foster, that I want you out of my house, out of my life as soon as possible—the sooner the better. I won't have a cowardly liar under my roof."

"Liar! Coward? You're calling me a liar *and* a coward?"

"You bet I am. All this bull about me using you and you using me is just that—bull. You got in a little deeper than you could handle, so you made all this up as an excuse to bail out. Well, if you haven't got the guts to admit you're scared to death of falling in love with me, then who needs you, that's what I'd like to know."

"Lady, you don't know what in the hell you're talking about."

"Oh, don't I?" She sauntered closer to him, hands on hips, nose in the air. "If you think for one minute I'm capable of what you've accused me of, then you either don't know me at all, or you've spent a good long while talking yourself into believing it. I loved you, Morgan, and you damn well know it."

A muscle in his jaw twitched. "You loved me?"

"That's right—loved. Past tense. I refuse to have any feelings other than disgust for a man who has to make up lies to worm his way out of a relationship with a woman."

She spun around again, and this time was able

to stalk off and leave him standing there in the yard. She made it as far as the shed before she realized how violently her knees were trembling.

Damn him!

Damn her!

Morgan pushed the back door shut, then leaned against it savoring the icy indoor air.

I want you out of my house, out of my life.

"You've got it, lady."

"You say something, Dad?"

Morgan jerked toward the sound of Wes's voice. He hadn't even noticed the boy at the kitchen sink. He stood away from the door and straightened his shoulders. "Find your brothers and sisters, then start packing. We're leaving. Now."

Wes just stared at him, his mouth open, his face pale.

With nothing more in mind than escape, Sarah threw a bridle on the Appaloosa and thundered over the hill, letting the wind in her face blow away the tears.

An hour later, sweat-soaked and gritty from her ride, she walked into the house and followed the sound of young voices into the living room. There she halted in horror. Boxes and sacks and piles of clothing and toys strung from the living room out onto the front porch. Children's clothing. Children's toys. Dizziness assailed her, and she leaned against the doorframe to steady herself.

This was it, then. They were really leaving.

Rob came in and picked up a box. His cheeks

were damp, his eyes puffy, and he wouldn't look at her. He carried the box outside to Morgan's new station wagon, with its doors and tailgate yawning wide, like so many open mouths ready to swallow up the children and take them from her sight, her arms, forever.

A sudden commotion upstairs drew her attention. A scuffle, a thud, and a muffled oath, the latter undoubtedly from Morgan.

"No! No! I don't wanna go!" Angie shrieked. The small child flew down the stairs and catapulted herself at Sarah's legs.

"Angie!" came Morgan's harsh cry from the top of the stairs.

Angie sobbed against Sarah's thighs. Sarah squatted and wrapped the girl in her trembling arms. "It'll be all right, Angie sweetie, you'll see."

Angie roared her grief against Sarah's neck. "He says we have to go away!' Another sob shook her whole body. "I don't wanna go away, S-Sarah, I don't wanna go! Don't let him take me. Don't let him take any of us!"

Sarah squeezed her eyes shut and tears raced down her cheeks. How could she explain such a cruel happening to such a small little girl? She couldn't even explain it to herself. *Oh God, Angie, I'll probably never see you again, and I love you so much, sweetie, I love you!*

She held Angie and rocked her and tried to soothe her with nonsense words about a new adventure, an exciting new home, new friends. All of that meant nothing to a child who could remember no other home, no pair of comforting arms other than the ones that held her right then, and Angie sobbed even harder.

"Wes, get your sister."

Sarah's eyes flew open. Morgan's hard brown gaze locked with hers for an instant. Then he turned and picked up the last two sacks of clothes and carried them out.

Wes looked at her, his face etched with misery. He blinked his eyes, and his lips trembled. "Sarah . . ."

Sarah clenched her jaws to keep from wailing. She held out an arm to Wes. The boy rushed forward and dropped to his knees at her side and threw his arms around her shoulders. The three of them sobbed together.

After a moment Sarah forced the two away from her. "Hey," she said, her voice shaking. "What are we all blubbering about? We'll see each other again. Maybe your dad will even let you come back for a visit once in a while."

She knew the words weren't true, but if the lie would help them all get through the next few minutes, it was worth it.

Wes straightened and squared his shoulders. He picked a still-sobbing Angie up and clutched her to his chest. Without looking at Sarah again, he whispered a tortured good-bye and went out the door.

Against her better judgment, but unable to do otherwise, Sarah followed him. When Connie, Rob, and Jeff saw her, they piled out of the car and ran to her, tears streaming down their faces.

Oh God, oh God.

Sarah grabbed them to her desperately, holding them, crushing them, kissing them. One sob forced its way from her throat, then she viciously clamped down on her emotions. Her tears were only making things harder for the children.

"Will you write to me and let me know how you're getting along?"

All three of them sobbed and nodded. "We will. We'll write."

"Go on then," she forced herself to say. "Your dad's waiting for you. Behave yourselves and mind your dad."

"We will, Sarah."

Morgan stood beside the car, stony-faced and silent. His own eyes were suspiciously damp as he watched the twins and Jeff pull reluctantly away from Sarah's arms. He knew they were hurting. Hell, this wasn't any picnic for him, either. But what choice did he have?

They couldn't stay here and live with Sarah just because it was easier on all of them. His children needed a permanent home, one provided for them by their own father. Someday they'd come to understand that. Maybe.

When they were all finally in the car, Morgan started the engine and headed down the drive. The dogs followed the car for over half a mile before turning back.

All the kids had quieted except Angie, who still sniffed and hiccuped. A moment later she wailed. "What if Speedy Tur-Turtle comes back? He won't be able to f-find me!"

In the rearview mirror Morgan saw Jeff put his arm around Angie. "I let Mr. T go last week. Speedy'll probably find him. They're probably playing together right now."

"Y-You think s-so?"

"Sure," Connie said. "They're probably playing together right now."

A moment later Angie screamed. Morgan slammed on the brakes. The car swerved on the rutted dirt road and nearly landed in the side ditch before he regained control.

"Jingles! I left Jingles! We have to go back for Jingles!"

Morgan slumped in the seat. Jingles. The bear with the bell in its ear.

Angie screamed and wailed at the top of her lungs. Morgan's hands squeezed the steering wheel until his knuckles threatened to pop through his skin.

"We'd better go back, Dad," Wes advised.

Morgan looked at his oldest son. "You really want to go back and tell Sarah good-bye again?"

Wes looked away quickly. A moment later he turned in the seat and pulled Angie up front and sat her on his lap. "Hey, Angie." Wes's soft, deep, calm voice was a direct contrast to her high-pitched, frantic wailing. "I thought you left Jingles there on purpose."

"I d-did n-not! I want Jingles!'

"Hush now, and listen to me." Miraculously, she did just that. "I thought you left Jingles so Sarah would have someone to talk to, so she wouldn't be all alone and sad without us."

"But he's afraid of the dark." She sniffled again.

"Sarah knows that. She'll take good care of him. Maybe she'll send him to you."

"H-how?"

"She could mail him," Rob offered.

"But she'd have to put him in a box," Angie protested, her tiny fists rubbing holes in her eyes. "It's dark in a box, an' he's ascared of the dark."

Morgan eased the car back onto the road and drove on.

"Sarah'll think of something, Angie, don't worry," Wes told her.

Sarah stood in the sudden silence and watched until she could no longer see their dust rising from the road. It took everything she had to keep from doing like the dogs and running after the car.

She finally forced herself to go back into the house. The first thing she saw, lying abandoned—as abandoned as she felt—halfway up the stairs, was Angie's Jingles. Blinded by tears, she stumbled up the stairs and sprawled on her face, clutching the stuffed bear to her chest and crying for all she was worth.

Rita found her there an hour later.

With the exception of Morgan's children, Sarah had never been part of a large family. But neither had she ever lived totally alone. She'd always lived in the old farmhouse with at least one other person.

Until now.

Now she was alone. If it weren't for the animals, she'd have gone crazy. But the animals either took more care or caused more work than ever before, both because she was the only one to do the work and because of the heat and drought.

The chickens, of course, had stopped laying due to the heat. That was normal for this time of year. What wasn't normal was for their drinking water to get so hot, even in the shade, that it required changing two or three times a day. The poor birds stuck to whatever shade they could find and just sat there panting. There was nothing more pitiful than to see a chicken panting.

Unless it was a cow trying to keep cool in such impossible heat. Shade wasn't good enough for Edna. Neither was fresh drinking water. She spent her days standing belly deep in the ever-shrinking duck pond. She got herself so covered in mud that Sarah was forced to wash her off thoroughly each time she got ready to milk her, just to keep the mud out of the milk pail.

The animals weren't the only ones to suffer from the heat. It sapped every ounce of energy from Sarah. By the time she'd been outdoors ten minutes her arms and legs felt like they weighed a ton.

The days dragged on, with no relief in sight.

But the nights were the worst. The nights all alone in the big, silent house. She missed the noise and laughter of happy children. She even missed the tears and tantrums of unhappy ones.

And God help her, she missed Morgan. She missed him the way he'd been for those few short days when they'd been happy together. When she'd had such hope for the future.

Now her future loomed before her, a giant black vacuum threatening to gobble her up the first time she let down her guard. But she wouldn't let down.

She'd get through this somehow. It wasn't in her to give up.

The children were gone. Morgan was gone. Those were facts she could do nothing about. She didn't even have any idea where they'd gone. Probably back to Washington, D.C., for all she knew. Morgan had no ties in Oklahoma. It wasn't likely he'd stay in this part of the country.

So what she had to do was take Rita's advice and cheer up. Just as soon as she figured out how.

The hours of darkness stretched out forever, seeming to never end, except with the relentless arrival each morning of the scorching sun.

The garden began to shrivel. To avoid boiling the plants where they stood, she had to water at night. In the early mornings, when it was coolest—but unfortunately also the most humid—she hauled compost out of the bin and piled it around each plant as mulch to help conserve moisture and lower the soil temperature.

The surrounding towns and cities were already rationing their water supplies. Sarah knew she, too, would have to be careful.

Of course none of her precious water was going to be wasted on such frivolous things as washing the car or filling up a swimming pool. The yard and flower beds would have to suffer, too. Sarah would not waste water on decoration. Her only water source was her well. If that ran dry, that was it. She couldn't call the city and complain. She couldn't write her congressman. Her water wasn't politically controlled. It was strictly a gift from the earth, from Mother Nature herself. And Sarah would not abuse it. She had no desire to run out.

The water in the ponds would serve the animals—they drank it all the time. But it was bright red and filled with algae. Even by boiling it, she couldn't drink it, cook with it, or even bathe in it.

The dogs didn't care if the yard turned brown. They just dug it up. In every spot that fell in shade anytime during the day. They dug all along the house and under every tree and shrub, digging for cool.

The only things to thrive in the heat were grasshoppers, horseflies, squash bugs, and wasps. The wasps left Sarah alone, as long as she did the same with them. The squash bugs hid under the mulch and sucked the life out of the squash plants, yet without the mulch, the plants would die anyway.

The horseflies, most of them longer than her thumb, thrived on the heat. They didn't bother Edna much—she was so covered in mud they couldn't get to her. But the horses were another story. As much as she hated using chemicals, Sarah ended up using a strong repellent on the horses. Their swishing tails just weren't able to keep the vicious flies from biting.

The grasshoppers, normally kept under control by the chickens and ducks, thrived. The chickens and ducks had no energy to waste on anything other than keeping cool. Every step Sarah took outdoors brought at least a half dozen enormous grasshoppers leaping through the air. Most of them landed on her. And clung. She brushed them off and went on.

Would it never end? The heat, the despair, the loneliness?

According to the weathermen on television, there was no drought relief in sight.

Fluffy white clouds rolled across the sky, mocking the parched land. Daily, Sarah grew more jealous of those clouds, up there being tossed around by some upper level wind. Down on the ground, there was no wind.

It was the one thing you could count on in Oklahoma. The only time the wind did *not* blow, and blow hard, was when the temperature reached one hundred. When a person would kill for just a hint of breeze.

Come winter when the mercury dipped below freezing, there'd be wind aplenty, howling through the chimney and the bare trees.

Rita made it a point to drive over—"It's too damned hot to hike that hill"—to share iced tea and gossip, and to generally try to cheer Sarah up. Sarah loved her for it. And it did help a little. Not much, but a little.

After two weeks, Rita threw her hands in the air. "I give up," she sad. "You obviously don't want to be cheered. You'd rather drag around this big ol' empty place and feel sorry for yourself. But what I want to know is, exactly who is it you're pining for, the kids or their father?"

Sarah blinked at her best friend's outburst. Feeling sorry for herself?

Of course that's what you're doing, you dope.

"Oh," she said.

"Yeah, *oh.* You haven't even tried to get on with your life, and you know it."

Sarah took a deep breath. "You're right. But just how do I go about doing that?"

"Do something," Rita said adamantly. "Go shopping, buy a new dress. Hell, you've got the money, buy a new car. Spending money has definite therapeutic benefits, you know. Just don't you dare buy anything *useful*. Think frivolous."

The smile that popped out on Sarah's face felt strange. "Therapeutic?"

"Therapeutic. Trust me. I'm your best friend. I know about these things. The last time Barry and I had a fight I bought a hundred and twenty dollars worth of new underwear. Made me feel like a million bucks."

Sarah forced a smile and refrained from reminding her friend that she, Sarah, had no one to model new underwear for. Then she bit her tongue. *There you go again, feeling sorry for yourself.*

"All right," she said with a decisive nod. "I'll go shopping tomorrow. Where shall we go?"

With regret, Rita told her that she and Barry would be leaving tomorrow for an overnight stay with her parents in Tulsa. "But don't let that stop you. You never minded going it alone before, so you go without me. 'Shop till you drop,' as they say."

EIGHT

The tall growth that lined the road—mostly sunflowers and sumac—was covered in a heavy, clinging layer of red dust. Everything along the road looked one uniform color—and the color was dry. Sarah knew that even if the wind should deign to blow, the dust would stick. Nothing but a long hard rain would wash the leaves green again. And there was no rain in the forecast.

Sarah decided to skip the nearby Shawnee Mall for this shopping expedition in favor of distance. Today she needed a little distance. She'd go to Oklahoma City. Instead of heading south to pick up the interstate to take her there, she went north and took old U.S. 66. The old two-lane highway had lost its status as "America's Mainstreet" years ago to interstate highways, but she still loved to drive it. The curves and traffic and small town speed zones required concentration. It helped take her mind off the box in the backseat.

Last night she'd located all the things the children had left behind when they'd packed. She had no idea where the Fosters were, but she hoped Tom Cartwright would be able to get the things to them.

In her purse were the passbooks for the five separate savings accounts she'd set up for the children. Every dime the state had sent for their keep had gone into those accounts. With the investments Gary had left her, she'd had no need for the extra money to feed and clothe them.

An hour and a half and eighty miles after leaving home, she finally pulled into the giant parking lot at Oklahoma City's Quail Springs Mall. She'd picked this mall because it was the farthest from the farm. Maybe the time away from home would help her with the pretense of "getting on with her life."

The first thing she noticed after leaving the sweltering one-hundred-plus August heat for the cool, air conditioned mall was the incongruity of the outdoor heat and the fall and winter clothing displayed in every window.

What on earth was she doing here? She had no place to wear any new clothes.

Shop till you drop.

Well, she could window shop, she supposed. But that in itself, according to Rita, was not necessarily therapeutic. It was the spending of money that cleansed the soul and gave new meaning to life. The *frivolous* spending of money.

Sarah rolled her eyes, hitched her shoulder bag to a more comfortable position, and trudged off in search of something to spend her money on. Maybe she could find a new purse. She could use a new pair of rubber boots for wading around the chicken yard muck, but the only place she knew to buy the kind she liked was the feed store in Meeker.

Purse? Rubber boots? You're not thinking frivolous, Sarah. Think frivolous.

"Well," she muttered under her breath, "I don't need a new toothbrush, so if I bought one, that'd be pretty darned frivolous, wouldn't it?"

Good gracious! she thought a half hour later when her wanderings took her past the Frederick's of Hollywood store. *Talk about frivolous!*

She had no idea what the . . . ensemble? . . . was called, but it was short and skimpy and see-through black, and had fringe and lace and—*my God!* —slits in the most . . . *amazing* places. That poor mannequin—to be exposed like that in front of thousands of shoppers!

A bark of laughter flew from her throat before she could stop it. She could just see herself in that getup, out feeding the chickens and milking the cow. Her calf-high rubber work boots would add just the right touch.

Sarah shook her head and walked on. What the hell was she doing here, anyway?

Lunch. That would be frivolous, considering the amount of food in her freezer. She'd buy lunch.

With that decision out of the way, she felt much better. Until she came to the display window filled with children's clothing.

Her heart gave a little stab of pain. The emerald-green corduroy pinafore with rows of white eyelet ruffles peeking out from beneath the hem looked as if it had been made especially for Angie.

Tears formed in Sarah's eyes. She blinked rapidly. One escaped and rolled down her cheek. With a muffled cry, she turned her back on the dress and wiped the tear away.

Lunch. She was supposed to eat lunch. It would be doubly frivolous now. She wasn't a bit hungry. She took the elevator down to the lower level and strolled past the food stands, finally deciding on a baked potato smothered in beef stew.

When compared with the size of potatoes she grew in her garden, the one they served her made her envious of the soil and climate conditions that could produce such a monster. But the stew wasn't nearly as good as her own.

After tossing the empty cardboard container and plastic fork in the trash, she squared her shoulders. Rita would give her the third degree about this excursion, and Sarah had better have something *frivolous* to show for it.

Wouldn't Rita just choke if Sarah went home with that little number in Frederick's window! By golly (as her father would have said), she'd do it! She'd lay out cold cash for that shimmery scrap of nonsense and teach Rita to send her out for something *frivolous*.

Morgan sighed and rolled his shoulders. He hadn't expected it to be easy to step into the roll of single parenting, but he hadn't counted on the children's total lack of cooperation, either. Back-to-school shopping, according to some magazine article he'd read somewhere, was supposed to help ease the disappointment of summer's end.

It didn't seem to be working.

Nothing seemed to be working.

The kids had all been helpful enough in getting settled into the house they'd rented. All but Angie. But they were not the same happy-go-lucky children who'd run loose and free on Sarah's farm.

They were quieter, more serious, less joyful.

Then there was Angie. Angie, whose hand he held. Angie, who'd refused to speak one single word, to him or anyone else, since resigning herself to the loss of Jingles—and Sarah—in the car the day they'd left the farm.

"I smell popcorn," Connie said.

"Yeah. I'm hungry. Can we eat, Dad?" Rob was always hungry.

"Yeah, lunch."

Morgan agreed readily. At least they were showing some enthusiasm about *something*. It was the first he'd seen from them in two weeks.

They checked the store "map" and located the string of fast food stands on the lower level. Naturally, each of the kids wanted to eat at a different stand. He dug out the roll of ones he carried for just such an occasion. "Get what you want and we'll meet at that table in the corner," he said. They scattered like dust in the wind.

While keeping an eye on the others, he leaned down to Angie, whose hand he still held. "What would you like to eat?" Naturally, instead of speaking, she pointed. "A corn dog?"

She almost looked at him. But at the last second she turned her head away and nodded up and down once.

Morgan sighed. At least it was communication. Sort of.

"Three corn dogs, please."

The two of them met the others at the large corner table. Food disappeared in a flash. Morgan had a time getting all the mustard off Angie's face and hands. She sat through what her face practically shouted was torture without a sound. He wished she *would* shout. Cry. Talk. Anything.

But no, not his Angie. She wasn't about to utter a word.

Ten seconds later she made a liar out of him when she tried to pull her hand from his. Incredibly, he saw her lips move. He leaned down. "What is it, Angie?"

With her eyes focused on something across the huge, vaultlike dining area, she whispered, "Sarah." Well, he might have known the first words out of her mouth in two weeks would be about Sarah. Before Morgan could respond, she called out loudly, "Sarah! Sarah!"

Morgan and the children looked all around but saw no one who resembled Sarah. "Sarah's not here, sweetie," he said. "It must have been somebody who just looked like her."

Angie strained against his hold, her eyes darting frantically from stranger to stranger. After a long moment, she sank back into her chair, dejected.

"Come on," Morgan said while rising from the table. "Let's go back upstairs and look at that green dress again, Angie. Maybe you'll want to try it on this time," he urged.

He had to give a tug on her hand to get her to follow him.

"Yeah, Angie," Connie said. "We could get a green ribbon to match for your hair. Wouldn't that look pretty?"

Morgan, grateful for Connie's attempt, pulled her to his side and hugged her.

They took the elevator to the upper level; the kids liked its outer glass wall. Except Angie. She hid behind Morgan's legs and refused to look.

They'd barely made it through the crush of people trying to get on the elevator while they were trying to get off when Angie nearly broke loose of his hold.

"Sarah!"

Morgan's heart ached for the child. He knew she missed Sarah terribly. They all did. All but him, that is. He didn't miss her. Of course he didn't miss her.

But Angie's seeing Sarah in every other stranger was already wearing on him. A dull throb started behind his eyes. "It's not Sarah, sweetie."

"Sarah!" she said again stubbornly. She tried again to break from his hold.

"Angie, stop that."

"No! Sarah! Sarah!"

Again she tried to pull free from his hand. "It's not Sarah, Angie," he said firmly.

"Sarah! Sarah!"

Morgan looked helplessly at his other children, who looked helplessly back at him.

He got the shock of his life a moment later when Angie turned to him and sunk her sharp little teeth into his hand. "Ouch!" He immediately let go of her.

And Angie took off through what must have looked to her like a sea of legs. To Morgan it was a sea strangers. And a small child alone among hundreds of strangers spelled trouble. "Angie!" He and the other children took off after her at once.

The things I put myself through just to amuse Rita, Sarah thought, still feeling the heat of the blush as she left Frederick's. She tucked the package under her arm to conceal the bold logo as much as possible. With her luck, some pervert would spot it and follow her home.

She was three stores away from Frederick's when she thought she heard someone call her name. She turned, but spotted no one familiar in the throng of back-to-school shoppers. She headed once more for the exit.

A minute later she heard it again, louder this time. Someone—some young someone—was screaming her name. She spun around and gasped. "Angie!" Sarah squatted and opened her arms, and the child of her heart flew to her, nearly knocking her down upon impact. "Angie, Angie!"

"Sarah! I knew it was you, I knew it!'

Sarah stood up with Angie in her arms. The two of them hugged and laughed and cried as nameless strangers rushed past.

"It *is* Sarah!"

Sarah looked up and saw all of them then. Jeff,

Connie and Rob, and Wes. And behind them, their father, looking grim-faced as ever.

Her heart fluttered its way up into her throat. Grim-faced or not, the sight of him still made her knees weak.

For an instant, their eyes met. And for an instant, she thought she saw in his eyes the same emotion, the same yearning that made her own throat ache.

But the look was gone so fast, surely it had never been there at all.

He was the first to look away.

"See?" Angie boasted, drawing Sarah's attention. "I *told* you it was Sarah!"

Sarah hugged and kissed each child. Lord, but it seemed like years instead of just two weeks since she'd seen them, touched them. A huge lump rose in her throat. "Oh, I've missed you so much."

Morgan never knew precisely why he chose that moment to open his big mouth, or why he chose those particular, cruel, untrue words. It was a combination of things, most likely, the first being the cheerful chatter pouring from Angie's lips—Angie, who hadn't uttered a sound in two weeks. He rubbed the spot on his hand where she'd just bit him.

Good God, his own daughter bit him!

But maybe the real reason he wanted to break up this little party was the uninhibited way Sarah and Wes were holding each other.

It was happening again, only this time it was much, much worse. He was jealous of his own children; jealous of the love Sarah felt for them;

jealous of the freedom they had to put their arms around her and know their deep affection was returned.

Acknowledging the jealousy only made things worse, for it brought on the inevitable guilt. And the guilt made him want to lash out at the source of all his problems. So when she said she'd missed the children, he opened his big fat mouth.

"Missed the monthly check from the state, don't you mean?"

Sarah and Wes broke apart abruptly.

"Dad!" Wes cried.

The sheer fury that sparked in Sarah's eyes—Sarah's *gray* eyes—was enough to make him want to put his hands up in defense. He'd faced spies and murderers and hostile armies with a calm most of his fellow agents had envied. But this woman made him want to seek safety.

An instant later he wished he had. With no warning at all, her right fist connected with the exact spot in his chest guaranteed to knock the breath out of him. And it did. He doubled over in stunned agony.

Sarah flexed her fingers and turned her back on him. "I'm sorry you all had to witness that. I'm sure I shouldn't have done it, but . . ." She fished around in her purse and pulled out the items she was searching for. "Here are the passbooks to your savings accounts." She glanced over her shoulder to make sure Morgan was listening. "All the money sent from the state since you came to live with me is there. It's yours. I have some other things out in the car that you left behind. I'll leave them with Tom Cartwright."

With a last heartrending look at each precious face, she said, "I love you."

Then she turned and ran for the nearest exit.

"Sarah, wait! You dropped—"

She didn't hear the rest of Wes's words as she shoved her way out the doors and into the parking lot.

It wasn't until her tears had dried, an hour after she got home, that she remembered she'd forgotten to take the box to Tom's office, and she realized what Wes had been trying to tell her as she'd run out of the mall.

Oh, my God!

She'd dropped the package from Frederick's!

Morgan sat on the edge of the bed, arms folded, feet braced wide apart, and stared at the offending sack lying on his dresser across the room. A muscle in his jaw twitched in steady rhythm to the grinding of his teeth.

It damn sure hadn't taken her long to get over her professed love for him, had it. Two weeks, and she's out shopping at Frederick's of Hollywood. The filthy word he muttered would have singed her ears.

Damn her!

A woman without a man in her life did not buy things like . . . *that*.

No, sir, it hadn't taken her long to get over him at all.

Who would have thought a practical, down-to-earth, wholesome farm girl like Sarah Collins would wear— A sudden picture shot into his mind of Sarah wearing that scrap of nothing he'd found in the sack. With a groan, he tried to banish it. Because the picture was too sharp, too vivid. Too arousing, even in his anger. And entirely too painful.

He fell back on the bed and covered his eyes with his arm.

I love you, she'd told the children.

The words whirled in his mind, echoing softly. For a moment he allowed himself the pain and pleasure of remembering the first time he'd heard those words from her, whispered breathlessly in the throes of passion.

He could still feel her skin beneath his fingers, soft and silky. Her fingers on his skin, taking his breath away. The taste of her. Those little sounds she made that drove everything but her from his mind.

Damn her!

The minute Sarah heard tires crunching gravel in her driveway she knew who it was. When Morgan stepped out of his car into the cloud of dust he'd brought with him, her heart, in spite of her will, thundered at the mere sight of him. When he rang the doorbell she made herself count to ten before opening the door. She pushed the storm door open and stepped back, but he just stood there. The look in his cold dark eyes sent shivers down her spine.

"Didn't waste any time filling your bed, did you?"

Sarah gasped. "What—"

"Don't bother looking so surprised. I'm not. Surely you haven't already forgotten I have first-hand knowledge of just how passionate you can be. Tch, tch. You wound me, Sarah, if you've so quickly forgotten our few nights together. Here," he said, ramming the Frederick's package against her chest. Reflex made her grab it before it fell from her lifeless fingers. "Trust me, your newest lover will be thrilled with your purchase."

Sarah stared, unable to believe or even understand the hateful words pouring from his mouth. She watched, dazed, as he turned and walked back to his car. When he reached for the door handle, something inside her snapped.

"Damn you, Morgan Foster!" she screamed.

"No, Sarah," he called back, "damn *you*."

"Jealous? Oh come on, Rita."

"I'm serious," Rita cried. "Of course he's jealous. Damn jealous. Why else would he drive all the way out here and say what he did?"

Sarah rubbed at the dull ache in her forehead. It was two days since Morgan had come flinging his accusations and her sack. Two lonely, miserable days. When Rita had come over an hour ago, Sarah had found herself pouring out all the gory details.

"Sarah, my girl, in case it hasn't occurred to you, a man who cares nothing for a woman does not go to the trouble he went to just to hurt you. It means he's hurt, too, and jealous, and he's striking back the only way he knows how."

Sarah sighed and dropped her hands to the kitchen table where she and Rita sat over sweating glasses of iced tea. "The only thing about that man that could possibly be hurt would be his pride. He doesn't have to care anything for me to be upset at the thought of my being with another man so soon after he left."

"What I don't understand," Rita said, puzzled, "is what set him off in the first place. What made him decide you were only after the kids?"

Sarah shrugged. "He just said he knew I'd do whatever I had to do to keep them with me."

Both women watched Rita draw wet circles on the tabletop with the bottom of her glass. A moment later, they both raised wide, startled eyes to each other. Both remembered the night of the rodeo. And the phone call.

"You don't suppose—"

"Could he have heard—"

They both spoke at once, then stopped.

"That has to be it!" Sarah exclaimed. "He was fine, happy even, until on the way home from the rodeo that night!'

"Oh, my God."

But even though they thought they knew what had caused the problem, neither knew what to do about it. Rita went home a short time later feeling responsible for the pain in Sarah's life.

Sarah paced the floor and wondered. Could it be true? Could he have overheard her flippant remark to Rita? Could those few careless words have caused him to think the worst of her?

If so, he hadn't had much faith in her character

to begin with, she thought, sudden anger coursing through her.

What was she supposed to do now? Grovel at his feet and beg for a chance to explain?

The anger left as suddenly as it had come.

Yes. She'd like to explain. She could use the box for an excuse. She'd really like the children to have the things they'd accidentally left behind. He hadn't given her time to even think about giving it to him the day he'd returned her package.

But she didn't know where he lived, and his phone was unlisted. How was she ever going to get the chance?

Morgan swirled the last remnants of Jack Daniel's around in the bottom of his glass. With a curse, he realized it was barely past noon. Did this mean he was turning into a lush? He put the glass to his lips and drained it.

He'd enrolled the kids in school today. They would start classes in just over a week. All but Angie. He had yet to find a day-care center for her. He hated the thought of sending her out among strangers, but she needed the contact with other children her own age.

At least she was talking now—to her brothers and sister, if not to him. Hell, she wouldn't even look at him anymore. It would be useless to keep her with him all day every day when she refused to have anything to do with him.

He wondered idly why he'd made the commitment to stay in Oklahoma City when he'd never lived west of the Appalachian Mountains in his life.

Stupid question, buddy.

Yeah. Stupid.

He was still in Oklahoma because Sarah was in Oklahoma. There was something unfinished between them. He didn't know what it was. A final, more definite, more painful break with her, maybe. How things could be more final, more *over*, he had no idea. But something still remained to be done.

He just wished to hell he knew what it was. He knew he had no intention of ever seeing her again, so why was he still here?

One thing he knew he had to do that he'd been putting off for weeks was talk to Wes. He'd never straightened out that argument they'd had about Sarah. Morgan shouldn't have come down on Wes the way he had.

He found Wes in the den, watching television with the rest of the kids. Wes looked at him over the heads of his younger brothers and sisters. Morgan nodded toward the door, and Wes followed him. They went to Morgan's bedroom and shut the door. This was one conversation Morgan didn't want overheard by the others.

"What do you want?"

Morgan sighed. This wasn't going to be easy. Nothing had been easy between him and the kids since they'd left the farm. But this was no time for subtleties. He took a deep breath and plunged right in. "Why did you think Sarah and I were . . . were . . ."

"Sleeping together?"

At least there was no sarcasm in Wes's voice. Morgan was relieved for that much, anyway. "Yeah."

Wes shrugged. "I woke up hungry one night. Sarah's bedroom is next to the kitchen. I heard voices."

"Just because you heard us talking in her room, you think we were . . ."

"Sleeping together. Yeah, well . . . it was three in the morning."

Morgan paced back and forth at the foot of the bed. What he really wanted to know was how Wes felt about his father sleeping with his foster mother. After a long silence, he finally asked.

Wes studied the floor and shrugged again. "I thought it was great. I thought it meant you two were . . . that we'd be staying, that we'd be a real family."

Morgan read the sincerity, the pain, in his son's face. So, Sarah had been right after all. Wes plainly didn't have . . . designs on her. He'd never been so relieved in his life. But that didn't alleviate the pain Wes was feeling. And it didn't answer all the questions. "Who else knows?" he asked.

Wes's head jerked up. "Nobody. You think I'd talk about something like that? The others are just kids, Dad."

Morgan smiled for a minute, then frowned. "I'm sorry for the way I treated you when you asked me about all this. I shouldn't have jumped on you the way I did."

"Did you . . . love her, Dad?"

"The point is, son, she didn't love me."

"You're crazy!'

Morgan looked down his nose at Wes. "I beg your pardon?" He wasn't used to being criticized, and most definitely not by his own children.

Wes grimaced. "Sorry. But, Dad, you're wrong. Sarah must have loved you. She wouldn't . . . well, you know, if she didn't love you. Sarah's not like that."

Morgan nearly sighed out loud. Maybe she had loved him, or at least thought she had. "Well, it's beside the point now. It didn't work out. I'm just sorry you and the kids had to get caught in the middle. I know you wanted to stay there. But I couldn't stay, and I sure wasn't going anywhere without you."

The phone rang once, then stopped.

"Dad, it's for you," Rob hollered from the other room.

"Morgan here."

"Morgan, Benson. We finally got word."

"Coop?"

"He's been captured."

NINE

Sarah checked her face in the hall mirror for the dozenth time in as many minutes. Did she look all right? Was her hair okay? She checked the buttons down the front of her blouse—no T-shirt today. Would they recognize her out of uniform?

Wes had called nearly two hours ago. They'd be here any minute and it was all she could do to keep from bursting out in tears at the mere thought of seeing the children again.

She could still hear Wes's voice, so tentative, so unsure, asking if they could stay with her for a couple of weeks while their father went out of town on business. Good Lord! Had he thought she'd tell him no?

For every time she'd looked in the mirror in the last few minutes, she'd also wondered what kind of business would take Morgan out of town. And how the children felt about it. The first thing he'd done when he'd come home was promise he'd never leave his family again.

Was he back with the agency? Did it have something to do with all those phone calls he'd made to Washington? Or that report he'd sent?

Maybe, *please, God*, maybe he had a different job now, and this was just a simple business trip.

She made another dash upstairs to make sure their bedrooms were clean and ready, then back down to the kitchen. The chickens were thawing, two pitchers of tea occupied the top shelf of the fridge, and a tea towel covered the plate of just-made chocolate chip cookies.

When she returned to the living room, Morgan's station wagon was pulling to a stop out front.

Kermit and Miss Piggy circled the car, yelping and yapping and nearly putting dents in the doors, they were wagging their tails so hard. The car doors popped open and all five children bailed out with shrieks and laughter, to be greeted by swiping tongues and adoring eyes. "Kermy! Piggy!" they cried.

Sarah stood looking out the storm door, both hands pressed over her heart to keep it from bursting with joy.

Then Moran stepped out of the car, tall and lean and oh so welcome to her eyes, even if his mirrored sunglasses did hide half his face. Her heart threatened to pound its way right out of her chest. When her next breath finally came, his name came with it. "Morgan."

She opened the door and walked outside. *Morgan.*

"Sarah, Sarah! We're back, Sarah!'

The children converged on her and she took them into her embrace and hugged and kissed and welcomed them home. But her eyes stayed glued to Morgan.

Before they even unloaded their clothes and toys from the car, the kids ran off, dogs and all, to see the horses.

Morgan hadn't moved. Sarah took a deep breath. If he wouldn't come to her, then she'd go to him.

"Hello, Morgan."

Stone-faced, he nodded. "Sarah."

"Can we talk?"

He shrugged. "Sure."

"Is this a new job you've got that's taking you out of town?"

"No."

"Then it's your old job again?"

"Yeah."

"Are you going to answer all my questions with a single word?"

A muscle in his jaw twitched. "What do you want, Sarah?"

"I want you to talk to me!" she cried in frustration. "Why do you have to go away?" she demanded. "Where are you going? Is it dangerous? When will you be back? Should I have the kids start school here or wait for you to take them home again? Talk to me, Morgan. And take off those damned glasses so I can see your face!'

Morgan grinned suddenly. He pulled the glasses off. The grin, combined with the teasing glint in his eyes, sent Sarah's heartbeat into overdrive. "My kids never mentioned this particular side of your personality," he said.

"Your kids seldom see this side. They aren't nearly as mule-headed as their father. Are you going to answer my questions or not? And why are you standing out here in the heat? Come in the house," she ordered.

"Yes, ma'am," he drawled.

Inside, Sarah motioned for him to sit at the kitchen table while she poured them each a glass of iced tea. "Okay, now talk."

Morgan took a long swallow of tea, then held his glass with both hands. "What's with the tough act, Sarah?"

Sarah pursed her lips. "How else do you suggest I deal with a stubborn, obstinate, long-eared mule of a man who makes a habit out of taking tiny scraps of information—out of context, I might add—and jumping to all sorts of erroneous conclusions?"

He sat back in his chair. "I presume you mean me?"

"If the shoe fits, as they say."

"What's this all about, Sarah? You've obviously got something on your mind, so why don't you spit it out?"

"I've got a lot on my mind. But first I'd like you to answer my questions."

He glanced at his watch. "I don't have a lot of time. I've got things to do before I leave in the morning."

"Morgan, please? I need to know."

Morgan lowered his gaze from hers and thought, *Why? Why do you need to know, Sarah? Why do you seem to care? What game are you playing now?* But he didn't voice any of his questions. Instead, he found himself answering hers.

"All I can tell you is I have to go back to

Central America for a couple of weeks, maybe a couple of months, I don't know. Just before I got home, the agency sent a friend of mine down there to find me. By then I'd already left the country. He's still down there looking for me, only now he's managed to get himself thrown in prison. I have to go get him out."

"Why do *you* have to go? I thought you quit? Can't they send someone else?"

He looked up from studying the tabletop to see the anxiety in her big gray eyes. Something in his gut twisted. Damn! What kind of hold did this woman have on him? He'd sworn to have nothing more to do with her, and now all he wanted to do was take her in his arms and kiss her until her eyes turned blue again.

He cleared his throat. "No one knows the locale, the terrain, or that particular prison like I do. And I owe him. Coop saved my butt more times than I can remember when we were in the army together."

"Do—" Sarah stopped and swallowed. "Do the kids know where you're going and why?"

"Most of it. Here," he said, pulling a piece of paper from his pocket. "If you need anything while I'm gone, call this number."

Ignoring the paper, she reached across the table and grasped his hand. Every nerve ending in his body went on alert.

"You'll be careful, won't you?"

She couldn't do this to him. Damnit, she couldn't! She couldn't start him thinking she cared. He pulled his hand from hers and stood. "I'm usually careful."

Sarah would have said more, but the back door burst open and children flooded the kitchen.

"Go get your things out of the car," Morgan told them. "It's time for me to go."

"Don't go yet, Daddy," Connie begged.

"He can't go till we get our stuff outa the car, silly," Jeff told her.

"Gee," Rob said, grinning. "That could take a while. You're liable to be here all night, Dad."

"All right, you jokers," Morgan said. "Hop to it and unload that car."

"Now, Morgan . . ." Sarah pushed back from the table and stood with the children. "I'm sure they have plenty to do right now. They can unload the car after supper. You can stay that long, can't you? I'm frying chicken. You know how you love my fried chicken."

He wanted to tell her no. He didn't know what game she was up to this time, he only knew he didn't want to play. The sooner he got away from her, the better. His nerves couldn't take much more.

But when he looked down into the eager faces of his children, he knew he was lost. He'd stay for supper.

After supper the children managed to drag out the unloading project until bedtime. Morgan promised to come upstairs and say good night as soon as they were in bed.

Sarah knew this was her last chance to talk to him, and she only had a few minutes. Then he'd be gone. "Morgan, I—"

A sudden, loud sobbing cut her off. She and Morgan dashed for the stairs. Sarah was half a step ahead of him when they reached the girls' room. Angie was hugging her pillow in one arm and Jingles in the other, and sobbing for all she was worth.

"Angie, baby, what's wrong?" Sarah knelt beside the bed and Angie slid into her arms, dropping the pillow and bear in favor of Sarah's neck. Sarah felt Angie's hot, desperate tears scald her through the material of her shirt. "What is it, sweetie?"

"I di-didn't mean to be bad," she cried between sobs. "I won't be b-bad anymore. Don't let my daddy go away. I'll be good, I pro-promise!"

"Oh, honey."

Angie raised her head to wipe her nose on her arm and saw Morgan standing there. She sobbed harder.

"Come here, baby," he said, emotion making his voice rough.

Sarah stood and handed Angie to him. The child clung to him and cried even harder. "I won't be bad no more, Daddy, I love you. Don't go, Daddy!"

He clenched his eyes shut, his face contorted with pain. "Baby, I'm not going because you were bad. It's only a short business trip, that's all. You couldn't do anything bad enough to make me leave you, sweetheart."

"But I did, I did!" With her face pressed against his shoulder, her words were muffled but clear. "I was a bad girl. I let Speedy pee on you and then I wouldn't talk to you . . . an' I . . . oh, Daddy! I bit you!'' After another sob she said, ''An' once, when you weren't looking, *hic*, I even stuck my tongue out at you. I won't do it no more, honest I won't. I didn't mean to be bad. I'll be a good girl, I will. Don't go, Daddy, don't go.''

Sarah, with her own heart breaking for Angie's pain, watched helplessly as one emotion after another crossed Morgan's face. This was tearing him apart, and there was nothing she could do. It was between him and Angie.

With her own eyes none too dry, she tucked Connie into bed and gave Morgan and Angie some time alone. She could hear the soothing tone in his voice as he comforted his youngest child. With a pang, she longed for that same comfort for herself.

She said good night to the others then went downstairs. It was nearly a half hour before Morgan joined her.

''Is Angie okay now?''

In a gesture of weariness, Morgan rubbed a hand across his face. ''I think so.''

Sarah hurt for him. To have to leave his family after having them for such a short time was hard enough. But the scene with Angie had drained him. He looked ten years older than he had at supper. ''Sit down for a few minutes. You're in no shape to drive just yet.''

He sat on the couch. ''Got any coffee?''

''I'll put some on.''

As soon as it was brewed she brought him a cup. If she was ever going to talk to him, it was now or never. She was afraid he'd leave as soon as he drank it.

"I don't mean to add more confusion to the night, but there's something I want you to know before you leave."

He kept his gaze locked on his cup of coffee, but she saw the muscles in his shoulders tense. "What's that?"

"That you're wrong about me."

He looked at her then, coolly. "How so?"

She sat sideways on the opposite end of the couch. "In a lot of ways, really, but mainly that you'd think I'd use you, and that you think I . . . well, that I've been . . . seeing another man."

"Sarah, I don't—"

"No, Morgan, let me finish. I don't want you getting on that plane in the morning and taking off for God-knows-where thinking that about me. I've been with two men in my whole life. And one of them I was married to for twelve years."

He just looked at her, his gaze boring into hers, and it was impossible to tell what he was thinking. His voice came out harsh. "Come off it, Sarah. You don't owe me any explanations, but a woman who sleeps alone doesn't buy things like . . . *that*."

"It was a joke, Morgan. A silly, stupid joke. That's all. Rita was trying to cheer me up after you left. She made me promise I'd go out and buy something completely useless. Frivolous. I saw that thing in the store window, and I thought, now there's frivolous if I ever saw it."

"A rather expensive joke, I'd say. I saw the price tag."

"And that's another thing I want to get straight. Not that my finances are any of your business, but you seem to be under the impression I needed that money the state sent for the children's care. For your information, I don't need it; I never did. Gary was an accountant. Investments were his hobby. I earn more money off the investments he left me than I could ever spend on myself."

Morgan shrugged. "So I was wrong about the money."

"And about . . . the other."

He sighed. "All right, that, too."

"And I wasn't using you, Morgan."

He quirked a brow. "You weren't?"

"No. I wasn't. Sure, I didn't want you to take the kids away. But you know me better than that. You know I wouldn't have . . . slept with you, made love with you, or even, as you put it, have run-of-the-mill sex with you, for such a cold-blooded, calculated reason. You know I wouldn't."

He stared at her a long moment. "Then why did you?"

"Because of this." She reached out and took his hand in hers. She felt the tremors clear down to her toes. The look in his eyes said he felt them, too. "Because of what happens between us whenever we touch. Whenever we kiss. There's nothing run of the mill about it, and you know it. You're just too stubborn, or too scared, to admit it."

"Scared?" He jerked his hand from hers and looked away. "What do I have to be scared of?"

"You tell me."

Morgan's gaze met hers once more. His eyes were dark and wary. Was that pain she saw there?

"Damn you, Sarah," he said harshly. His hand

shot out. He grabbed her arm and hauled her onto his lap. She went willingly, for it was where she belonged. "Damn you," he whispered as his lips took hers.

The kiss was fierce and hungry and desperate. Sarah reveled in it. He crushed her to his hard, wide chest as his hands ran feverishly, restlessly over her back, her face, tangling in her hair.

Morgan blocked everything from his mind but the feel of her, the taste of her. Just then it didn't matter if she'd used him, didn't matter that he didn't trust her. The only thing he knew or cared about was having her, possessing her, making her his. He wanted to brand her with his heat, as she was branding him.

He needed her. God, he didn't want to, but he needed her. Desperately, wholeheartedly, with every fiber of his being, he needed her to need him.

He tore his mouth from hers and gasped for breath. She planted kisses along his jaw and down his neck, then answered his silent prayer. "I need you, Morgan, I want you. Don't go yet. Don't go."

He rose from the couch with her in his arms and kissed her fiercely. "No," he said with effort, with feeling. "Not yet." He kissed her again as he stalked through the kitchen to her room. "I won't go yet. God help me, I can't."

They tumbled onto the waterbed with arms and legs and lips clinging. The gentle motion of the bed, combined with Morgan's lips, made Sarah's head spin. "I was so afraid," she whispered against his lips.

"Of what?" His fingers tore at the buttons on her blouse.

"Of never seeing you again, of never feeling your touch or hearing your voice."

Morgan paused and searched her face. Even in the darkness he could see the truth shining in her eyes.

She clutched him to her and buried her face against his shoulder, muffling her words. "But I'd rather not see you again at all if it means you have to go back to that place."

Morgan couldn't let himself think about the import of her words. He tucked them away in a corner of his heart, to pull out and examine later, when he didn't have the distraction of her in his arms, when he'd need the words to get him through what lay ahead of him in the jungle.

He reached for her buttons again and jerked them free. He tossed the blouse to the floor. The bra followed it. Then he pulled back and stared, awed by the beauty of her flesh, her breasts.

Sarah arched her back, inviting him to touch, to taste, but he only looked. Even so, she felt her nipples harden. Morgan moaned. She took his hand and brought it to her breast, then pulled his head down. "Please," she whispered. "Please."

He hadn't realized he'd been holding his breath until it came out in a rush with her name. "Sarah." He wanted to go slow, to savor every inch of her, to store her up in his memory for future reference. Future torment.

He only meant to brush her with his mouth. But at the first light touch of her beaded nipple against his lips, his brief flirtation with control collapsed and he took her into his mouth hungrily, greedily.

Sarah arched and gasped. When he suckled, she moaned. His lips and teeth and tongue tugged sharp, tingling sensations up from the very depths of her right out through her breast.

She jerked his shirttail from his pants and reveled in the heat of his satiny skin beneath her palms. He shifted toward her other breast. Before he closed his mouth over it, she pulled off his T-shirt. Then he took her other nipple like a starving babe. She cried out with intense, almost unbearable pleasure. She tried to undo his pants, but he held her so tightly she couldn't work the zipper.

Realizing what she wanted, and wanting the same thing, Morgan raised on one arm, without relinquishing the hard nub in his mouth, and yanked off his clothes and hers. Both of them gasped when heated skin met heated skin.

Then his hand closed over her mound. She thrust her hips into the air. "Yes," she cried. "Oh, Morgan, now. Please, now."

He felt her hot and wet and ready. "Yes," he said with a gasp. "Now."

He slid into her, hard and fast, burying himself completely in her silky depths. "Oh, God," he cried. "Sarah," he said, pulling back and thrusting again. "Sarah."

The tempo increased. With each thrust, she muttered something he couldn't hear over his own harsh breathing. But the harder, the faster he thrust, the louder her words, until he couldn't help but hear.

"I love you . . . I love you . . . I love you I love you I love you I . . . love . . . you!"

Her nails dug into his back, but he scarcely felt it. What he felt was the turmoil in her body as she climaxed beneath him, around him. He gasped with the fierceness of it. His own release came seconds later. And it was so powerful, so consuming it threatened to hold him forever.

Sarah lay with her head on his chest, listening to the solid beat of his heart. It was a sound she would never grow tired of. "When you get home, you and I are going to have a long talk." He loved her. She knew it. It was there in every touch, every kiss, in every moan. All she had to do was make him realize it, and accept it.

Home. The word sang in his blood. *When you get home* . . . This was home for him, in Sarah's arms. "We are?"

"We are," she assured him.

"About what?"

She raised up and brushed his lips with hers. His quick intake of breath was gratifying. The new, quicker rhythm of his heart matched hers. "About this." She kissed him slowly, thoroughly. "About what we do to each other. About why we can't kiss without ending up tearing each other's clothes off. About why that bothers you so much. About why you don't trust me."

He threaded his fingers through her hair and closed his eyes. "Sarah, I—"

"It's all right, Morgan. Well, I mean it's not all right that you don't trust me, but we don't have to talk about it now, tonight. It'll keep until you get home."

Morgan sighed and pulled her head back down to his shoulder. "I hated you, you know. Before I ever even heard your name."

Sarah forced herself to relax. "Why?" This was important, whatever he was going to say. He'd never shared his thoughts with her, only his feelings, and even then, only physically.

"Because of all the foster homes I grew up in. They were nothing like this. The people were nothing like you. I imagined my kids going through some of the things I experienced at the hands of foster parents and I was livid. I came here fully prepared to rescue them from some horrible existence. And the first thing I got was plastered with a tomato."

She heard the smile in his voice and grinned.

"It didn't take me long to realize you really cared for my children, and they worshiped you. And then, when I . . . when I started feeling things for you . . . things I shouldn't have been feeling, I watched you with the children, and I could see history repeating itself."

"History?" Sarah frowned. "What history?"

He was quiet for a long time. "My marriage."

"What does any of this have to do with your marriage?"

She tried to raise up, but Morgan held her against his chest. He hadn't planned on telling her any of this—he'd never talked about it before—but the words were there, ready to be said. But he couldn't look at her while he spoke, so he held her.

"When Joyce and I got married it was as much for convenience as for anything else. She was the up and coming darling of Washington society; I was a decorated war veteran. We looked good together, we felt good together, so we got married. I'm not sure we ever even thought in terms of love. Until the kids started coming."

A small ache grew in Sarah's chest at the talk of his wife.

"When Wes was born, you'd have thought we were the first two people in the world to ever produce a child. We were both pretty disgusting, I'm sure. When the twins came along, I thought Joyce would appreciate that I'd cut my hours at work so I could spend more time with her and the kids.

"I couldn't have been more wrong. She told me flat out that she didn't need me underfoot, messing up her schedule. Joyce loved schedules."

She heard the slight trace of bitterness in his voice and longed to comfort him. Yet she dared not interrupt, for fear he would stop talking.

"By the time Jeff was born I realized that 'underfoot' was exactly how she thought of me. She had the children she wanted, the social standing, her club meetings. She didn't need me any longer. That's when I took the job with the agency and started traveling."

Sarah wondered if he understood just how much his ex-wife had hurt him. How much influence the woman still had over his actions, his thoughts. "You think I'm like her? That I only want the children, and not you?"

With a hand to her chin, he lifted her face until she looked directly into his eyes. "I know you want me, Sarah. You've never tried to hide it."

She grinned. "You noticed?"

"I noticed." He grinned back. Then his grin faded. "I have to go soon."

"Morgan, I—"

"No," he said softly, pressing a finger to her lips. "No more talking, or I might end up making promises I don't know if I can keep. I can't make promises. Not yet. It's something I'm going to have to work out on my own. For now, just love me, Sarah, love me."

I do love you, her heart cried. But she pressed her lips to his and blocked the words. He'd heard them before. She'd told him; she'd shown him in every way she knew how. If he didn't believe her yet, then more words wouldn't help.

The knowledge was there, buried somewhere within him. It was up to him to find it, believe it, accept it.

Amid the tangled sheets, he rolled her on to her back and covered her with his strong, lean body. If this was all she ever had of him, she wouldn't spoil it now with worries. She gave herself over to the magic, the heat, the desire that flared between them.

Their bodies joined, and once again they drove each other over the edge, where fireworks exploded and time stood still.

But time didn't stand still. It was only an illusion carved out of wishes. The clock ticked away relentlessly until Morgan could no longer delay leaving.

God, he didn't want to leave her.

He tried to talk her into staying in bed, but she refused. She wouldn't give him up until the last possible moment. She stood with him beside the car in her father's T-shirt and her slippers. He was leaving. Her heart was even heavier than the hot, humid air that weighed on her chest like a load of bricks.

"Promise me you'll be careful," she said, sliding into his open arms.

"I promise."

His lips met hers, so tenderly she felt tears sting her throat.

"Take care of yourself, and the kids."

He gazed at her long and hard, as if trying to imprint her face firmly in his mind. She did the same. "Don't worry about us," she whispered. "We'll be fine."

"I've got to go."

"I know."

"Maybe when I get home . . ." He threaded his fingers through her hair.

"When you get home?"

He grinned slowly. "Maybe I can talk you into wearing that little black number you picked up at the mall." It wasn't what he'd meant to say, but it was safer, saner.

"You can count on it, mister."

Her throaty, teasing whisper nearly buckled his knees. He pulled her to his chest, felt her breasts against him, felt her heart pound. He kissed her then, one last time. Suddenly his own mortality tapped him on the shoulder, and he realized with startling clarity that, with what lay ahead of him on this trip, this could very well be the last time he ever held her.

Then, before he could do or say something he might regret, he pushed her away and got into the car.

Sarah bit her lip to keep from crying out. She grasped the door where the window was rolled down. He pried one of her hands loose and brought it to his lips. Her vision blurred.

When he released her, she forced herself to step away. He started the car, and, through a blur of tears, she watched him turn around in the driveway. He was leaving. Dear God, he was leaving.

He was a hundred feet down the drive. The brake lights suddenly glowed bright red in the night.

"Sarah?" he called out.

She would have run to him, but her knees trembled so badly she couldn't move. "Yes?" she called back.

For a long moment the only answer was the soft rumbling of the car's engine. Then Morgan called out, "I love you."

She moved then. She took one step forward, but the car sped off down the driveway and out onto the road.

"Damn you, Morgan Foster!' she screamed. "Now's a hell of a time to tell me!'

TEN

Sarah slowed the car and turned off the highway onto the dirt road that led to her farm. Clouds of dust billowed up behind the station wagon and hung in the air, adding another layer of red earth to the roadside weeds and trees.

She let the children's talk of school and teachers and renewed friendships ease her mind. She smiled as Wes talked about being allowed to go out for football in spite of having missed two weeks of practice.

Since Morgan had never answered her question last week, she'd gone ahead and enrolled the kids in school today, barely in time for them to start classes in two days with the rest of their friends.

She wondered what Morgan would say when he came home. The chances were better than average that they'd only have to start over at a new school in a week or two, but she hoped not. Oh, how she hoped not.

With what she and Morgan felt for each other, surely he'd want to stay. Surely he'd meant what he'd said as he'd driven off that night. She'd just have to hope and pray that while he was gone, he would make up his mind to trust her. And when he came home next week . . .

Only he didn't come home next week. Or the next. The third week of his absence, an official-looking envelope from the U.S. District Court arrived, addressed to her. In it was a document signed by a judge giving Sarah legal custody of Morgan's children until his return.

What did it mean? He'd be home any day, so why had he gone to all that trouble?

The drought hung on, and so did the heat. And Morgan didn't come home. Angie missed her brothers and sisters while they were away at school all day, and waited eagerly each afternoon for the school bus to bring them home. And every day, she asked when her daddy was coming home.

Sarah only wished she had an answer.

By the middle of September the high temperature during the day was all the way down into the midnineties! A regular cold snap, compared to August. But still no rain. And no Morgan.

While October was just as dry and grass fires plagued the state, the eighty-some-degree air was easier to breathe. But the ground continued to bake and crack, the grass continued to turn brown, the ponds—the ones that still existed—continued to shrink.

The duck pond was nothing but a dried-up mud hole. Edna and the horses moved on to the bass pond up the hill. The ducks and geese went with them. Sarah worried about that. The big bass pond held an unknown number of turtles. Barry and Rita had lost all their ducks last year. Turtles swam up beneath them, grabbed them by a foot, and pulled them underwater. Sarah hoped her ducks and geese didn't suffer the same thing.

Then there was the hay shortage. Because of the drought, there wasn't a bale of hay to be found anywhere in the county. After a few phone calls, Sarah discovered the same was true for the whole state, and beyond.

For her three horses and one cow—Tippy the goat didn't count; she'd eat anything—she didn't need much hay, but she needed *some* to get them through the winter. Barry, with his larger horse and cattle operation, was in much greater need.

In the middle of October, Barry hitched up his long horse trailer to the pickup and went looking for hay for his stock and Sarah's. He was finally able to purchase what he needed in Tennessee.

And through it all, Morgan's place at the table remained conspicuously empty. Sarah alternately worried about and privately raged at him. There'd been no word—not one. What could be taking so long? Was he all right? Was he hurt? Had he, God forbid, gotten himself thrown into that same prison he was supposed to be rescuing his friend from? If something wasn't wrong, then why wasn't he home?

And how dare he shout "I love you" and then just drive away. Did he really mean it? Why hadn't he told her sooner?

When he came home (and she wouldn't for a single minute let herself believe he wouldn't), would he be over his silly notion that she was only using him to keep the children?

Damn him. Where the hell was he?

During the first week of November, she'd had all the silent waiting she could stand. She called the number Morgan had left her. A young man answered. When she asked to speak to Mr. Benson, she was told he was "unavailable." She had to use Morgan's name to get the man to put the call through.

"Yes, Mrs. Collins, what can I do for you?"

"Mr. Benson?"

"Yes, ma'am."

"I'd like to know if you have any word about Morgan. Uh . . . Mr. Foster."

He had none. "But these things take time, Mrs. Collins. I'm sure if anything was seriously wrong, we would have heard. We'll let you know the minute we hear from him. It shouldn't be too much longer."

Sarah hung up the phone and stuck out her tongue, wishing the man with the too-smooth voice could see her. Ooo, that voice. "I'll bet in his last life he sold snake oil from the back of a wagon," she mumbled to herself.

With a heaviness pressing down on her spirit more firmly each day, she went through the motions of getting ready for Thanksgiving. Her heart wasn't in it, so worried was she about Morgan, but the children needed the distraction.

She bought a twenty-two pound turkey and started it thawing. The kids cut out giant turkeys and pumpkins from construction paper and decorated the house. Jeff traded two new pencils with a boy at school for three colorful ears of dried Indian corn. They would be the centerpiece on the dining-room table.

"Wow. We get to eat in the dining room?" Rob asked.

"Of course, dummy," Connie informed him. "It's a holiday. That's what dining rooms are for."

Sarah smiled. She knew that before the children came to live with her, they'd been accustomed to nightly formal dinners, for which they'd been required to "dress." It had taken them awhile to get used to her informal way of doing things, but now it was as if they'd forgotten linen napkins and ruffles and bow ties and not being allowed to speak or laugh during meals.

And she was glad.

The day before Thanksgiving she made Waldorf salad from her mother's recipe, steamed the sweet potatoes she would candy the next day, prepared carrot sticks and stuffed celery, and baked three pies: two chocolate and one pumpkin. She would have made the traditional mincemeat, but nobody, including her, would eat it.

She had tried, for weeks, not to let herself dream of spending this holiday with Morgan. She had honestly tried. But somewhere along the line she must have failed, for Thanksgiving morning found her even more depressed than usual.

She blamed her low spirits on the clouds. For three days, huge gray storm clouds had rolled across the sky. Rolled across, and kept on going, without releasing a single drop of rain, teasing the parched land with promises the clouds had no intention of keeping. The days were mild now, even though temperatures in the midseventies were unseasonably warm.

Sarah opened the oven door and checked on the turkey, then covered the rolls with a damp towel and set them near the oven to rise. Macy's Thanksgiving Day Parade blasted from the television. Later in the day it would be football. And that night the children would join Sarah in her own Thanksgiving tradition by watching the original (although colorized) version of *Miracle on 34th Street*. She didn't even have to look in the television listings to make sure it would be on. It was always on Thanksgiving night, without fail.

Aside from regular sports programs, there were three things a person could count on on television: *Miracle on 34th Street* on Thanksgiving night, *The Wizard of Oz* in the spring, and Elvis movies in August. Like clockwork.

"Yes!"

Sarah cringed at Angie's piercing scream. Connie and Rob were setting the table, and Angie was "supervising." Apparently there was a disagreement about something. There'd been a lot of disagreements among the children during the past weeks. They were tense and upset over their father's long absence. But instead of talking about it, like Sarah tried to get them to do, they preferred to take it out on each other.

And today she just wasn't up to it. This was supposed to be a holiday. A day families spent together giving thanks for the year's bounty. Petty quarrels had no place on a day like this.

With a sigh, she wiped her hands dry and headed for the dining room.

"He is, too!" Angie insisted, her hands on her little hips, her face set in mutinous lines.

"No, he's not," Rob answered.

"What's going on in here? I thought you were supposed to be setting the table?"

"We're trying to," Connie claimed. "But Angie keeps moving the plates around."

"Cuz you didn't bring enough. I told you, Daddy's coming home today. You gotta set a place for him, too."

Rob rolled his eyes. "He's not—"

"I think it's a fine idea," Sarah interrupted. "I think even if your father doesn't get home today, he'd be pleased we set a place for him."

"But he *is* coming home today, I know it, I know it," Angie insisted.

Sarah put her hand on the child's shoulder. "I hope you're right, honey."

But her hope was slim to nonexistent. If Morgan were coming home today, someone would have called her by now.

Forcing the moisture from her eyes, she helped Angie set the extra place for dinner.

Angie spent the rest of the morning dashing to the window every few minutes. It nearly broke Sarah's heart to watch the child's hope-filled face collapse each time she saw the empty driveway.

Rob spent the morning trying to filch food.

"Trying to feed the monster again?"

"But I'm *starving*," he claimed when Sarah slapped his hand away from the nearest chocolate pie.

"Eat a carrot stick."

"A carrot stick," he groaned. "Wait till Dad gets home. I'm gonna tell him you starved me."

Sarah pursed her lips and looked him up and down, ignoring the devilish grin on his face, settling on the expanse of white sock showing between the tops of his sneakers and the bottom of his jeans. "Yeah, you look like your starving. You've grown at least an inch since school started."

"An inch! You really think so?"

Sarah laughed. "I know so."

"Hey, Wes!" Rob bounded out of the kitchen. "Sarah says I've grown an inch. Come measure me."

A minute later she heard footsteps pounding up the stairs and laughed. There'd be a new mark on the inside of the closet door in Rob's room any second now.

Finally, at two o'clock, just as the children were positive they were in the last stages of fatal starvation, everything was ready.

"Everybody, come wash your hands," she called.

The announcement was greeted with a cheer and a rush to the sink.

"But we can't eat yet," Angie claimed. "My daddy's not here yet."

"I know, sweetie," Sarah told her, smoothing the hair back from Angie's face. "But I don't think he'll mind if we start without him, do you?"

Angie lowered her head and stuck out her bottom lip. "I guess not," she mumbled.

"Don't touch that food," Sarah warned as everyone scrambled to the table.

It was another of Sarah's Thanksgiving traditions. On this day, if not on any other, everyone at the table had to voice something they were thankful for before their plates were filled.

"Who wants to start?" Sarah asked.

"I'm thankful for all this food," Rob said, grinning.

"I'm thankful it's not so hot anymore," said Connie.

Jeff spoke up next. "I'm thankful we didn't have to go to that dumb old school in the city."

"Hey," Wes objected, "I was gonna say that."

"Well, I said it first. You have to think of something else."

"Okay. I'm not glad Dad's gone, but if he has to be, then I'm thankful he brought us back here."

Sarah's eyes misted over. She reached for Wes's hand and clasped it in hers. "And I'm thankful for each and every one of you." She let her eyes touch them all one by one. "I love you very much."

Across from Wes at Sarah's other side, Angie sighed. "I'm thankful my daddy's coming home today."

Sarah immediately lowered her gaze to her plate, not wanting the others to see her sudden tears. She wished, she prayed, that for Angie's sake alone, Morgan *would* come home today.

Sarah Collins, you liar. She wanted him home for herself, at least as much as for the children.

Finally, with all the thanks given, food miraculously began to disappear from the serving dishes and reappear on plates.

Before filling her plate, Angie crawled down from her chair. Sarah wanted to stop her, but couldn't. The child's hope would be dashed soon enough. Sarah couldn't bring herself to rush it. Angie went to the window and looked out for a long moment before turning back to the table.

She wasn't back in her chair long enough to get her plate more than half filled, when suddenly she sat up straight and whipped her head around toward the window. "He's coming, he's coming," she whispered.

"Angie—"

But the child ignored Sarah and jumped from her chair and raced to the window again. Her high-pitched squeal captured everyone's attention.

For one brief second Sarah allowed herself to hope. But then she clamped down on the futile emotion with force. If she didn't stop Angie from running to the window soon, everyone at the table would surely be in tears. "Angie—"

"I told you! I told you!"

Without even a glance toward the others, Angie tore away from the window and out of the room. The front door crashed open. Sarah's heart started pounding in her chest.

"It's him! It's him!"

Around the table, they heard the storm door swoosh open, then closed. They all stared at each other blankly for half a second. Then, as one, they pushed away from the table and ran for the door.

As Morgan slowed to turn into the drive, the cloud of dust that had followed him from the highway overtook him and rolled across the car. Then he was clear of it, curving up the gravel drive.

His heart had been pounding in his chest for the past twenty miles. As he let his gaze roam over the land, the house, he felt an easing in his chest. This was home. Home like he'd never known it before. It welcomed him with open arms, demanding nothing, giving him peace.

There had been times during the past weeks when he hadn't been sure he'd ever see this place again. He felt like getting down on his knees and kissing the ground.

He pulled the car to a stop, and before he could get the door open, Angie was flying out the front door toward him. He stepped out in time to catch her in his arms.

"Daddy, Daddy!" she cried. "I *knew* you'd come today, I knew it. But nobody believed me."

He blinked sudden moisture from his eyes. "They didn't, huh?" He held her to his chest, clutching her desperately even as she tried to scramble down.

"Dad! It's Dad!"

Morgan whirled and was engulfed in four more sets of arms. *Home!* Oh, God, it was good to be home. He hugged and kissed and laughed. They all chattered at once so he couldn't hear what anyone was saying.

Then he looked up, and there she was. *Sarah.* She stood on the porch with her hands clasped over her mouth.

The need that had never left him during the past three months rose up and threatened to overwhelm him. *Sarah.* Gently he eased himself out of his children's eager embraces. He didn't see them step back, didn't see them glance pointedly at each other, then at Sarah, then at him, didn't see the hopeful grins spread across their young faces.

All he could see was Sarah. She hadn't moved. She stood there, poised as if frozen in motion. He walked slowly toward her, a sudden fear knotting his stomach. Why didn't she move? Why didn't she come to greet him? Had she changed her mind? Did she no longer want him, love him?

He stopped at the porch steps and looked up at her. It was then he noticed the tears streaming down her cheeks. His arms raised tentatively. "Sarah?"

Sarah closed her eyes briefly, then opened them. He was still there. She wasn't dreaming. This wasn't some cruel hallucination come to torment her. It was him!

With a sound that was part sob, part laughter, she drew her hands from her mouth and flung herself off the porch and into his arms.

Morgan stumbled backward but held on tight. "Sarah." God, but nothing in his life had ever felt so good. He'd been wrong earlier. It wasn't the land, or the house. His home was Sarah. He closed his eyes and covered her lips with his in a blistering kiss, trying to make up for all the lost weeks, months, of being without her.

Yes, this was his home. Right here, in Sarah's arms.

The buzzing in his ears sorted itself out until he pulled his mouth from Sarah's abruptly and opened his eyes. He didn't even try to fight the grin that formed on his lips. He and Sarah were surrounded by cheering children.

Sarah laughed, and Morgan looked down into tear-filled blue-gray eyes. "God, I've missed you. All of you," he added, letting his gaze touch each child.

"Come on, you guys," Rob complained. "You can kiss anytime. The turkey's getting cold."

Sarah laughed again, then pulled Morgan's face down for one more short kiss. "Welcome home, Morgan." She kissed him again. "Now it's a real Thanksgiving."

When they kissed the last child good night and started down the stairs, Morgan took Sarah's hand in his. She gazed up at him with a look of such warmth and tenderness he felt his pulse quicken. Giving in to the tension and desire that had been eating away at him all day, he swept her up in his arms and practically ran to her bedroom.

Inside, he kicked the door closed behind him. With their eyes locked, he released her legs. She stood before him smiling softly. When he reached to cup her face, he wasn't surprised to find his hands trembling.

He lowered his head and kissed her gently—teasing, touching, tasting. Her soft sigh and quivering lips pulled him deeper into her spell. When her hands stroked his sides, a shudder ripped through him. He crushed her to his chest and took everything she offered. Her response reached down and touched his very soul.

When they came up for air, he leaned his forehead against hers. "There were times," he said hoarsely, "when the thought of holding you against me like this was all that kept me going."

Sarah, unable to bear being so far away from him, buried her face against his shoulder. "I was so worried about you. You were gone so long. Was it very bad?"

Morgan forced himself to relax. There was no point in burdening her with the horrors of the past weeks. He was home now, and the horror was fading. He chuckled lightly. "It's not easy trying to slip out of a Latin American country when the guy with you is a blue-eyed, blond-haired prison escapee."

From the lightness of his tone Sarah realized he didn't want to talk about what had happened, what had gone wrong, what had taken so long. That was fine with her. All she needed to know right now was that he was safe, and home.

"Speaking of slipping," she said, pulling away from his warm chest, "why don't you . . . make yourself at home, while I slip into something more comfortable?"

Morgan noticed the teasing glint in her eyes and the quivering of her lips. "What are you up to? I don't want to let you out of my arms for at least a year."

She stepped out of his embrace and grinned. "I'll hold you to that. But for now, humor me."

"If you'll kiss me first."

He reached for her and she fell against him, wrapping her arms around his neck. It wasn't just a kiss of lips, but of hearts and minds, bodies and souls. When it ended, it was impossible to tell which one of them was trembling more.

"You slip into something comfortable." His husky whisper started a melting sensation deep within her. "Then I'm going to slip into you."

Her response to the vivid picture that sprang into her mind at his words was to grab his shoulders to keep from sliding to the floor. When she could stand on her own again, she pushed away from him. She stopped at the bathroom door and gave him a slow, heated look over her shoulder. "That's something else I'm going to hold you to."

She was gratified by the low growl that came from his throat.

She flipped on the bathroom light and closed the door softly but firmly behind her. Her hands shook violently as she pulled off her clothes. When she donned the garment she'd hidden in the drawer earlier and looked at herself in the mirror, she gasped. And blushed.

Did she actually have the nerve to walk out of there in that?

Yes, she decided. She did.

When she opened the door and stepped out into the bedroom, Morgan was in bed, the sheet covering him from the waist down, his clothes piled on her dresser across the room. The look that came into his eyes as he slowly sat up made her heart pound.

Morgan felt his breath halt at the sight of her. He raised himself slowly, not even aware of what he was doing. Pulses all over his body, but in one place in particular, started throbbing. He couldn't count the times he'd fantasized about her wearing that little bit of black lace and fringe he'd found in the Frederick's sack, but the reality far surpassed his imagination.

The fringe shimmied with each breath she took, and when she inhaled, parts of her he couldn't wait to taste peeked through the two strategically placed slits in the see-through lace. When she raised a knee to climb onto the bed he caught a glimpse of the tiniest, most provocative pair of black lace panties he was ever likely to see.

And then he was grabbing her and rolling over her, touching and tasting, nudging a slit in the lace open to take a nipple into his mouth. When he slid a hand down to cup the heat of her, he found a third slit in the fabric and groaned. His control was lost, as lost as he was.

Sarah gasped as he made good his earlier promise.

Morgan gazed down at her peaceful face, flushed from two rather inspired sessions of lovemaking. "I love you."

Sarah opened her eyes slowly. It was there, on his face for her to see, in his voice for her to hear. She swallowed the sudden lump in her throat. "But do you believe me? Do you trust me?"

He brushed a strand of hair from her cheek. "With my life, Sarah. Forgive me for taking so long to know my own mind."

"Oh, Morgan." She threw her arms around his neck and planted a dozen little kisses across his face and neck. "I love you."

"But I'm giving you fair warning," he said a moment later.

Sarah sighed and draped herself across his chest. "About what?"

From beneath his pillow he pulled a triangle of black lace and fringe. "If you ever wear this outside to feed the chickens, I won't be held responsible for what the children or anyone driving down the road sees."

Sarah giggled, then stopped. "Listen," she whispered.

"What? I don't hear anything."

"Rain!"

Morgan clanged his spoon against the rim of his coffee cup several times before the crowd around the breakfast table quieted. He raised his brows in surprise. "It works," he said, looking at his spoon in wonder.

He glanced down the table and smiled at the inquisitive faces paused in various stages of eating. "Now that I have your attention, there's something I'd like to ask Sarah. Rob, if you could please hold off feeding that monster you call a stomach for just a moment, I promise this won't take long."

Six curious pairs of eyes rested on him. He looked into Sarah's eyes—Sarah's *blue* eyes, he thought with keen pleasure, knowing he'd chased the gray away.

"Sarah . . ." Suddenly a fear like he'd never known before threatened to choke him. In the next instant it vanished. There was nothing to fear here.

This was Sarah. This was right. This was inevitable. "Sarah, will you marry me?"

His question was met with four gasps, one childish giggle, and from Sarah, stunned silence.

She should have expected it, she realized, but somehow she hadn't. At least not this soon, and not at the crowded breakfast table with five eager witnesses. She felt tears, and she felt a smile starting somewhere deep inside of her.

"No!" Connie shouted.

Six pairs of stunned eyes turned to her.

"Connie?" Morgan said, shocked and bewildered by her outburst.

Seated to Sarah's left, Connie reached out and placed a hand over Sarah's mouth. "You're not supposed to answer him yet. I read it in a magazine. You're supposed to make him sweat a while first."

Morgan felt the muscles in his jaws tighten. He narrowed his eyes and glared at his oldest daughter.

Connie dropped her hand and laughed. "I think he's sweating. You can answer now."

Sarah glanced from Connie's smug expression to Morgan's furious glare and broke out laughing. "Yes!' she cried. "Yes."

Morgan let out the breath he'd been holding.

"All right!" Wes shouted.

"Can we eat now?" Rob asked innocently.

With lips twitching, Morgan nodded. "You may feed the monster."

"Gee, thanks, Dad. Could you pass the butter, please . . . Mom?"